PAGE EDWARDS, JR.

• THE SEARCH •
FOR KATE DUVAL

A NOVEL

Page Edwards

D0167377

MARION BOYARS
NEW YORK • LONDON

Published in the United States and Great Britain
in 1996 by Marion Boyars Publishers
237 East 39th Street, New York, NY 10016
24 Lacy Road, London SW15 1NL

Distributed in Australia and New Zealand by
Peribo Pty Ltd, 58 Beaumont Road, Mount Kuring-gai, NSW

Library of Congress Cataloging-in-Publication Data
Edwards, Page
      Search for Kate DuVal : a novel / by Page Edwards, Jr.
      1. Missing persons—West (US)—Fiction.   2. Family—West (US)—
Fiction.   I. Title.
   PS3555.D95S43   1996
   813'.54--dc20   95-13116

British Library Cataloguing in Publication Data
Edwards, Page
   Search for Kate DuVal
   I. Title
   813.54 [F]

ISBN 0-7145-3000-X Original Paperback

Typeset in 11/13pt Ottawa and New Brunswick
by Ann Buchan (Typesetters), Shepperton
Printed by Itchen Printers Ltd, Southampton

Page Edwards, Jr. was born in Gooding, Idaho, in 1941 and raised in Durango, Colorado. He received his B.A. from Stanford University and his M.F.A. from the University of Iowa's Writers' Workshop. He is the author of a book of short stories and seven novels. He lives with his wife Diana in St. Augustine, Florida.

A portion of this novel was published in a different form under the title 'A Civil War Romance' in *Journeys* (Volume 2, Number 2) by the Florida Historical Society.

THE DUVAL GENEALOGY

Carl Chase. Father of Helen DuVal by Susannah DuVal. Born in Tallahassee, Florida, 1846. Deserted the Eighth New Hampshire at Olustee, 1864. Died, 1869, of fever.

Volney Chase. Born in Tallahassee, Florida, 1846. Fought with the Eighth New Hampshire at Olustee, 1864. Married Susannah DuVal, 1869. No children. Died, 1869, near Otavalo, Ecuador, from miner's lung.

Susannah DuVal. Born in St. Charles, Missouri, 1850. Bore one child, Helen. Married Volney Chase in Tallahassee, Florida, 1869. Died in St. Charles from complications after childbirth, 1871.

Maureene DuVal. Born in St. Charles, Missouri, 1852. Not married. No children. Madam of a prosperous house in Cherry Creek, Colorado, 1867. Returned to St. Charles, 1870, died there in April, 1929.

Uncle Tom DuVal. Father of Eleanor and Maren DuVal by Helen DuVal. Born in St. Charles, 1852. Left for West Texas, 1867, where he raised and drove cattle. Not married. Appointed Secretary for the New Mexico Territory, 1906. Died, by accidental gunshot wound, in Santa Rosa, New Mexico, 1912.

Jacob Stockett. Born in Fernandina, Florida, 1865. Traveled west with 1880 silver rush and returned to Jacksonville, 1885. Moved to St. Charles, 1890. Two adopted children: Eleanor DuVal and Maren DuVal. Married Helen DuVal, 1890. Died in St. Charles, 1925.

Helen DuVal. Daughter of Susannah DuVal and Carl Chase. Born in Tallahassee, Florida, 1869. Lived in St. Charles. Two children, Eleanor and Maren. Married Jacob Stockett, 1890, after Eleanor was born. Died, 1893, St. Charles, in childbirth.

Joseph Hodges. Born, 1887, in Hodgesville, Indiana. Operated lumber mill in Oak Hill, Florida. Married Eleanor DuVal, 1910. One child, Cassandra. Date and place of death unknown.

Eleanor DuVal. Daughter of Helen DuVal and Uncle Tom DuVal. Born in St. Charles, 1890. Married Joseph Hodges, 1890; attempted divorce, 1910, claiming her husband had gonorrhea; divorce denied. Two children: Cassandra, 1906, and Eliott, 1911, by William Ramsey. Died of complications from syphilis, 1915, in St. Charles.

William Ramsey. Father of Eliott DuVal by Eleanor DuVal. Born 1891 in Golden, Colorado. Not married. Died in Golden, 1943, in a mine cave-in.

Maren DuVal. Son of Helen DuVal and Uncle Tom DuVal. Born 1893 in St. Charles. Died in New York City, date unknown. Called 'the boy' by the family.

Cassandra DuVal. Daughter of Eleanor DuVal and Henry Prewitt. Born in St. Charles, Missouri, 1906. Married John Pratt, 1929. Two daughters: May DuVal, 1930; Eva DuVal, 1940. Died from the effects of arthritis, 1975, in Denver.

John Pratt. Father of May DuVal. Born in French Lick, Georgia, 1910. Married Cassandra DuVal, 1929. One daughter: May, 1930. Owned turpentine camp in Georgia. Acquitted for manslaughter, 1943, in Telluride, Colorado. Lives in Mancos, Colorado, and operates a perpetual care cemetery with his second wife, Sally Prewitt.

Eliott DuVal. Son of Eleanor DuVal and William Ramsey. Born in Denver, 1911. Not married. One daughter: Eva, 1940. Died in Golden, Colorado, 1943, in a mine cave-in with his father, William Ramsey.

May DuVal. Daughter of Cassandra DuVal and John Pratt. Born in St. Charles, 1930. Married Carl Haffey, a trail packer, in Telluride, 1959. One daughter: Carla, 1960. Died, 1984, of cancer in Durango.

Eva DuVal. Daughter of Cassandra DuVal and Eliott DuVal. Born in Denver, 1940. One daughter: Kate, 1970. Not married. She lives on a fruit and vegetable farm north of Santa Fe, New Mexico.

Ben Cooke. Born in Palo Alto, California, 1958. Teaches comparative literature at Fort Lewis College, Durango. Married Carla DuVal, 1985. No children.

Carla DuVal. Daughter of May DuVal and Carl Haffey. Born in Telluride, 1960. Married Ben Cooke, 1985, Durango. No children.

Kate DuVal. Daughter of Eva DuVal. Father unknown. Born in Santa Fe, 1970. Died 1988, Durango, while horseback riding.

For Susan E. Barrett

• PART I •

• ONE •

I should have known when I first met her that Kate DuVal was leading a double life — her bright life as an alert and beautiful young woman who was popular with her college friends, and her dark one populated by her ancestors who obsessed her, those shadows in her past. It was remarkable how easily she could move from one world to the other, admittedly confusing them at times.

Early in our relationship, I took silent offence when she called me 'Uncle Tom' or 'Jacob Stockett' or 'John Pratt.' But when I learned those men were dead and not her previous lovers, I began to flatter myself, believing that she had found a place for me in both of her worlds — both in her past and her present — and therefore that I had become to her necessary and permanent.

She was nineteen, a freshman here at Fort Lewis

College in Durango, Colorado, when her ancestors took her away from me. How terrified she must have been to find herself caught by her family heritage, ensnared by something so bred in the bone that she was afraid that she would repeat the past. Then how much more terrifying it was for her to discover that she was inextricably trapped. In the end, she gave up resisting and began in earnest to imitate what her mother and her grandmother and her great grandmother had done to ruin their lives.

I have come to know those ancestors: her great great great grandmother Susannah DuVal and her husband, the Civil War veteran Volney Chase who died of miner's lung in Ecuador; her great uncle, John Pratt, the owner of a turpentine camp in French Lick, Georgia, and his wife, Kate's grandmother Cassandra DuVal; Uncle Tom DuVal, the cattle rancher, and his lover, Kate's great great grandmother Helen DuVal, and Helen's legal husband Jacob Stockett; Eleanor DuVal, her great grandmother, and her husband, Joseph Hodges, who gave Eleanor syphilis; there are, of course, many others. She knew them well, Kate did, these ancient ones. And, finally, it was these same ancestors who carried her away from me.

At one time I had faith that family made one's own life more safe; I once held family life in reverence; I was envious of those who knew much about their roots and family ties. Before I met Kate and came to know her ancestors, I did not realize that, for some, blood ties are a dangerous, self-destructive force in one's life. My grandfather killed himself, and my father probably did, too. The call of suicide runs in my blood, but I have no need to answer it.

However, in Kate's instance, this promising, eager, beautiful young woman was overtaken by the virulent influence of her own family's past. If she had not so followed, or been led by, the call of her own family's blood, she would be half way through her freshman year by now and, perhaps, she would have found the courage to remain in love with me.

In the end, no living person won Kate's heart. I tried hard to keep her love, and I'm certain that she did not leave me for someone else; she left me to join her family. I can only believe that. It is too painful for me to believe otherwise. I lost Kate to the ancient ones. What I don't know is if I helped her along to her end. Was I an unknowing catalyst? By enabling her to rely as much as she did on the past to understand her life, did I help to seal her fate? Was I her benign facilitator? At times I believe I was and I cannot bear such thoughts.

I am Graden Wells, age forty-five. Before I begin Kate's story, I must tell something of my own.

So far it has been a hard winter. Even as I write this, it is snowing. It has snowed steadily for four days this time, and I have been outside twice and only then to clear the path up to Flame's barn. This yellow trailer where I have been living these past few weeks, Kate's old trailer, is capped with five feet of light powdery snow and there has been no wind, just snow, falling snow. I am buried by snow.

I came here last August, lost and unhinged, for a month earlier my father had died. As his only heir, he left me his house in Old Town Albuquerque, which I have sold, a sizeable portfolio of blue chips and mining company stocks, and just over fifty acres of land on a lake in the mountains north of Durango, which he inherited from my grandfather. There isn't all that much lake property remaining in Colorado, or any-where else for that matter. The taxes were negligible because there was no access, the property being located at the far end of Electra Lake where there are cow trails and an abandoned stage coach road, but the deed contains an easement through Forest Service land off highway 550.

I wasn't certain what my grandfather used the land for, but know my father never bothered to look at it, for he had neither the time nor the inclination to settle down in the Southern Rockies and live in a log cabin. At first, I wasn't particularly interested in the area one way or another, but the investment banker in me said not to sell the site unseen, even though my father had no use for the property. When the deed passed on to me, I resigned from my job managing other people's money in Boston and took a room at the Silver Spur Motel on North Main. I had the land surveyed and assessed in preparation for selling it, working up a deal which would give me about a half a million in cash, less capital gains.

During my first days in town, I rode the little train to Silverton, spent some time learning about my grandfather at the public library where I read the newspaper of the time, and at Fort Lewis College where I found accounts of the city's beginnings and of the making of Electra Lake, one of the first man-made lakes in the state built originally as a hydro-electric source for the San Juan Basin. My grandfather, Randolph Wells, was one of the original investors in the power company and as such got a pick of the choice lake front property (rather, of property that would become lake front once the dam was finished, backing up Elbert Creek and enlarging Bishop's Pond). In 1906, he took fifty acres at the north end, built a cabin and lived there five or six years before, according to his obituary, he killed himself. I guess my grandfather's suicide turned my father sour on the property and everything that went with it, but that is one of the things I didn't have the chance to ask him before he died.

When my grandfather built his cabin, there was one hardware store in town, Jackson's, which is still in business. A 1906 issue of Durango's *Examiner and Herald* describes how Jackson and his employees built the Wells cabin on the vacant lot next to the store, outfitted and finished it to the owner's specifications, and then dismantled it and carted everything in ten wagons twenty-five miles up the Animas Valley and over what would become the lake bottom and reassembled it on site at the upper end. Others followed my grandfather's example, though a few built their cabins from Ponderosa pine logs cut at the lake. One of Jackson's employees was a fourteen-year-old boy, Sy Cooke, who served as caretaker while the cabin was being reassembled and later did odd jobs for my grandfather. I was anxious to meet Sy and to see what was left of Randolph Wells' cabin.

Durango's main street has a row of tourist shops, restaurants and bars. The Barrel appealed to me more than the Golden Slipper or the Iron Bucket. Ned, the bartender in The Barrel, knew of Sy Cooke and told me I could find him north of town at the Wranglers Bar-B-Que, where he and three others — and sometimes a young woman, Kate — had a western-chuck-wagon-style stage show.

At The Barrel is where I met Kate DuVal.

She swept in one Thursday afternoon during Happy Hour, wearing a long black skirt and a white blouse. She had black hair which hung, not straight to her shoulders, but in heavy curls. Her legs were long and slender and her mouth full, with bee-stung lips.

She stood behind a bar stool and began talking with Ned. There was no one else at the bar and eventually Ned introduced us.

'He wants to meet Sy Cooke,' said Ned. 'You can arrange that, can't you?'

'I might be able to,' she said, before moving off to circulate like a politician in the crowd of college kids.

When she cruised by the bar again, Ned said to her, 'Come on, Kate, you can at least talk to him.'

'I bet I'm supposed to know you or something,' she said, on the verge of annoyance. 'Are you a teacher?'

'I'm new here,' I said. 'I'm looking up some of my family history. My grandfather, actually.'

She leaned on the back of the stool next to mine but did not sit down.

'That's what I do,' she said, brightening. 'I was in Florida and Missouri this summer looking up mine. I learned a lot. It's funny what you can find out, if you look and ask. Like my grandmother Cassandra was friends with this guy Sy Cooke who told me tons about her.'

'Well, I'd be interested to know what Sy Cooke told you about your grandmother,' I said, 'And I'd like to meet him while I'm in town.'

'Give me a minute,' she said, 'I'll be right back.'

She returned to a group of women who seemed to be her friends. They looked over at me. One wiggled her fingers — Sarah McCall, her roommate, I learned later. Drinks were two-for-one for the ladies that night, and Ned said Kate liked Tequila Sunrises. So I got a small pitcher and found a table. She knew everyone, it seemed, and was at home in The Barrel. I waited and eventually she made her way back to me.

What she wanted to talk about was her stories. She became quite animated, retelling bits of what she'd written about the DuVal women — Maureene DuVal, Cassandra, May. And Eva, her mother.

She impressed me as vivacious and naive, eager and unrestrained, but not loose or sluttish. I was struck by her singular handsomeness and her vitality. She had a sort of swagger and shook her black hair now and again as if it were her mane. I was attracted by her energy and confidence. And when she talked, her eyes became brilliant and warm, a fire-lit turquoise blue. Her nose was broken once below the bridge during a girls' basketball game. It was the broken nose which made her handsome rather than beautiful. She often wore an

Indian necklace of silver and turquoise — a squash blossom necklace made by a Navajo, a gift from her mother.

If I had not been interested in her stories, she wouldn't have given me the time of day. She did most of the talking. Yet, at one point, she interrupted herself to ask, 'What is it you want to find out about your grandfather?'

'Why he built a cabin here,' I said quickly. 'Sy Cooke is supposed to have helped him.'

The Barrel was noisy and crowded by this time, but Kate made no move to leave our table. She was absorbed, not in me necessarily, but by the tales themselves. They excited her, and my interest excited her even more. She was young, enthusiastic; child-like, really. And when she had been a child, she must have listened to the adults around her and absorbed most easily what she was not supposed to hear, the dark confessions, the secrets, the sins revealed in whispers. She knew her family secrets. And she set her stories in the dark shadows, the hidden world of her female ancestors. She told me that her grandmother was the family's most recent storyteller, not including herself. And from her Kate learned scandalous tales such as how her grandmother's grandmother, Susannah DuVal, had loved two brothers at the same time during the Civil War.

'I was visiting my grandmother Cassandra when I was eight or nine,' she said. 'And she showed me her collection of letters and deeds and telegrams and diaries. Each one held a story, and she told them to me one by one. It was awesome, and right then I realized that my ambition was to become a storyteller. What I'm going to do is keep adding stories to my notebook for as long as I can and then I'll pass them to my daughter or my niece or to someone who will continue them. It was Aunt May who got me started, really. She collected the family papers after my grandmother Cassandra died and passed them on to me. I feel sad for May; she had a happy marriage — there aren't many in my family. She died of liver cancer. I loved her, but her life seemed too boring. Sy Cooke almost died when she did. That was something. They both almost went out at the same time.'

'You know him fairly well, then' I asked.

'He's like a grandfather to me,' she said, 'and was like a father to Aunt May. But, he's never liked my mother. She's too wild for him, that's what I've always thought.'

'When Sy Cooke was a boy, he worked for my grand-father, Randolph Wells.'

'Oh, so that's who Randolph Wells is, your grand-father. He built a cabin at the end the lake not far from Sy's. I've been up there lots of times.'

'Perhaps you'll show it to me sometime.'

'No problem,' she said. 'I can borrow a couple of horses from Uncle Carl. He's an outfitter.'

While we were waiting for our second pitcher of Sunrises, Kate asked me to hold out my hand — the left one — and she closely examined the ring finger.

'You're not married,' she said. 'There's no indentation where you took your ring off.'

'Some men don't wear wedding rings.'

'You look like the faithful type who would, to keep the women away.'

'No,' I said. 'I'm not married. I was. Not anymore. And, I did wear a ring.'

'Married men are such a disaster.'

'How so?' I asked.

'My grandmother Cassandra married John Pratt from French Lick, Georgia. He didn't tell her that he thought he was still married to someone else because no one ever found his first wife's body after she let a train run into her. Grandmother Cassandra told me that one night at John Pratt's turpentine camp when they were in bed, Pratt's wife's ghost came into the bedroom. Can you imagine that? The ghost shouted at him, demanding that he get that ugly woman out of his bed. Cassandra wasn't ugly. Also, my great great great grandmother Susannah married a Civil War soldier, Volney Chase, but at the same time she loved his brother. She was never sure who her daughter Helen's father was. Helen's my favorite — she's my great great grandmother, the one who loved her uncle. Helen married someone else, but didn't ever stop seeing her uncle Tom.'

Ned brought the new pitcher and I poured us each a glass.

'How on earth do you know all this?'

'I'm interested. As I said, my grandmother Cassandra left some papers. Before Aunt May died, she helped me sort them out. And earlier this summer I went to Missouri and Florida to look up more records and stuff. Mom treated me to that trip. And I've talked a lot with Sy, who still loves my grandmother. I pick things up. I guess, I'm like a magnet when it comes to this stuff.'

'I'd like to meet Sy,' I said to her again.

'Sy? Sure, I can arrange that. I'll call him later. He lives with my cousin Carla and her husband, my English teacher. Actually, Carla is the best settled of all of us. She and Ben are like two peas in a pod. Much better settled than my great grandmother Eleanor was, that's for sure.'

'All these people,' I said. 'How can you keep them straight? You must have a soap opera running in your head.'

That offended her. She finished her drink and set the heavy glass down hard on the table.

'It's not a soap opera,' she said, her eyes blazing with anger. 'It's who I am. It's important.'

'I meant it as a compliment,' I said.

'I'm sure you did, but who wants her family to be called that. And, besides, they aren't that hard to keep track of.'

'Forgive me,' I said. 'I got carried away.'

'If you live with it, it's easy to keep track of them.'

She quieted down. I saw her mind shift subjects. 'What do you want with Sy, anyway?' 'Some family stuff of my own,' I said. Then I explained in more detail why I was there. She listened thoughtfully. She appeared interested. I liked that about Kate; she was a good listener and not just a one-note person, totally wrapped up in herself. At first impression, I thought Kate was just another one of the pretty college girls in The Barrel. The type who was well-liked, fun but not too silly, the usual intelligent young woman, but one with an animal-like grace and poise, well able to take care of herself. It was when she began to tell her stories that I became captivated by her.

On and on Kate and I talked that night.

The crowd gradually cleared from The Barrel and she went back up the hill to campus with her friends from school. I felt abandoned when she left me that night, standing on the sidewalk in front of The Barrel watching her lightly walk away to catch a ride with someone. First her black skirt disappeared in the darkness and then her white blouse, and she was gone.

Later, in my room at the Silver Spur I found that Kate stayed with me, rather, both Kate and her stories did. I can't tell you who else was in The Barrel that night or how the drinks tasted or what time it was when I fell into bed. What I do remember for instance was how deeply Kate's great great grandmother, Helen DuVal, loved her uncle Tom.

The next morning I ate a light breakfast of coffee, tinned fruit, and dry toast in the Silver Spur Cafe and returned to the room to gather my notes. The telephone began to ring a few seconds after I opened the door, causing me to think that I had set off a security alarm. It was Kate calling to invite me to meet Sy Cooke and to hear her sing that night with the Wranglers at Fort Wilderness.

•Two•

I arrived at the big stockade gates of Fort Wilderness early, hoping to talk with Sy Cooke before the show began. Inside, there is an imitation western town and a huge eating area with rows of picnic tables and a stage at one end. The cooking is done in the barn over a massive gas stove. There preparing the evening meal were three of the four Wranglers — Rudy Slavia on barbecue; Pete Thomas on spice cake and biscuits; and Joe Capo on beans. Neither Sy Cooke nor Kate had arrived yet.

'Kate, when she does show up, is always eager to help with dinner and the dishes,' said Capo, who had a faint English accent. 'A typical young girl in many ways, full of energy. She has a busy social life which doesn't include us most of the time. Lately, Katie has shown some interest in playing Western music on her guitar.

I do hope she's serious. Sy's offered her a place with us, if she doesn't start playing country or gospel. You see, the girl was polished by the schools back East, but she has a clear voice and holds a tune. Her fingers are right for the guitar, not too short and fat, and I've got her so she picks out a pretty recognizable "Ghost Riders" while I play the sweet potato. She harmonizes without making her voice sarcastic or nasal and sings like she means it. That's how the Wranglers sing; we mean it, old boy. We do only Western, pure Western, not country western, not rock country, not country blues.'

While I waited for Kate, I listened to the group warm up with a three-part, off-kilter version of 'Cool Water.' Pete kept time with a whisk in his mixing bowl and Capo tapped on a can of beans. In less than an hour they would serve dinner to three hundred and seventy-six.

Sy came in a few minutes later, introduced himself, and announced that Kate would be there for the show. 'She usually gets here in time to whip the frosting for the spice cake,' he said. 'Tonight she'll take over on string guitar. Capo, will you work the sweet potato. That's if she gets here. My guess is she's with some guy getting her heart broke again.'

During the peak tourist season in summer the chuck wagon at Fort Wilderness, which is meant to reproduce the chow fed to the cowboys on the Chisholm Trail, handles as many as four hundred at six-fifty a head, running them like cattle through a food line of beef-in-sauce, beans, biscuits, coffee, spice cake and apple sauce, all slopped onto a tin tray that conducts the food's heat so that you burn your hand if you don't put it under the compartment holding the apple sauce.

Sy Cooke and the Rocking Bar Wranglers play Western music as pure and clear as only a handful of men can now play it, directing their songs to women, to home, to horses, to the country. When you close your eyes and listen to them you swear that they are huddled around a campfire with nothing behind them but open prairie, horses and cattle.

The Wranglers are: Pete Thomas, from a family of West Texas cattlemen; Joe Capo, whose father and his father were chuck wagon cooks out of Magdalena, New Mexico; Rudy Slavia, with Bavarian blood and twenty years of longhorn experience near Borax, Nevada; and Sy Cooke, the son of a school teacher from Durango, who began riding the New Mexico-Arizona cattle trail at seventeen. They are a rare breed, sons of the frontier, who dress in their everyday clothes for a gig. Boots. Spurs. Indian belts. Jeans. Chaps. Ten gallon Stetsons. There's not a phony in the bunch.

The show was half finished when Kate, carrying her guitar case, came to my picnic table toward the back. She waved discreetly to Sy and sat next to me while the Wranglers finished 'Cool Water' and segued into a song I had not heard before — 'Slow Fires'. The lyrics told of a man who had lost his love, but who still burned for the beautiful woman.

'That's my favorite,' Kate said. 'Sy wrote it about my grandmother Cassandra DuVal. He fell in love with her when he was younger than I am and has loved her ever since. She got married to someone else — John Pratt — and Sy still loved her; and she had my Aunt May and my mother and he still loved her; and then she died in Denver and he loves her still.'

'She must have been some woman.'

'Oh, she was. Get him to tell you sometime. And if he won't, I will. Did you meet him yet?'

'Briefly before the show. I was hoping to see him afterwards.'

'That won't work. He sells tapes after. You'll never tear him away from that. It's best if you catch him at his place. There's no show on Tuesdays.'

'He seems like a busy man. Lots of brands in the fire.'

'Oh, Sy's eased off a bit,' Kate said, tapping her boot to the music. 'Still, this past summer season, he was always the first one to arrive at Fort Wilderness, all saddled and ready for the breakfast riders. Just after sunrise he and Rudy lead the trail riders from the stockade out of the river valley toward the east up Missionary Ridge. Up in the hills, Pete and Joe have a fire going and cook eggs and biscuits and sausages and bacon and enormous pots of coffee. I love the smells of breakfast — wood smoke, coffee, bacon — all mingled together. After breakfast the four Wranglers lead the dudes off through the pines to race the train. They're a gaudy lot usually. You should see the different hats and shoes they wear riding.'

As she spoke, Kate tapped the table to the last verse of 'Slow Fires.'

'When the narrow-gauge train appears down the valley, smoke belching from the stack, its whistle cues Sy's horse, which comes alive and prances. Sy does not have to spur his almost white palomino, just release the reins slightly, and the animal takes off at full gallop, running low and smooth after the train.

'Sy waves his hat. I love that. You know, he's almost eighty, but in the distance on his palomino it seems to me that he has no age. He is a man on a horse riding easily across the wide meadow after the train. I will always remember him like that. A man on a palomino, waving his hat, chasing a train that's pulling a line of yellow passenger cars.

'I might write a song about Sy,' she said.

'It sounds like you already have one started,' I said.

'Even now, running a tourist attraction,' she continued, 'and playing the fiddle in a western band, Sy still lives as well as he always has, no slower — at least not by his lights — no less vigorously, than he lived at thirty or fifty. Sy will always run at full throttle, right up to the end.'

The sad love song was over now and Sy announced that there was a young person in the audience tonight whom he especially wanted us to hear, if she would please step up on stage. At that, Kate said that she hoped to see me around and took her guitar from its case and walked down between the rows of picnic tables to the stage where she took the melody from Capo and he switched to the sweet potato alternating with the tub bass.

Kate was relaxed before the audience of barbecue eaters and certainly the Wranglers acted pleased to have her up there. She was, at the very least, a swell piece of cheesecake in her turquoise boots and tight black jeans with her cherry and mahogany Gibson guitar. She looked like the person for whom the cowboy songs were written, she was everyone's San Antonio Rose.

Kate was as talented as Capo said she was. A natural before a crowd. She sat on a stool and sang, tossing her hair now and again so she could see her guitar's frets. Her voice was pure and sad. I was struck by how competent she seemed to be at everything she tried. Beautiful, talented, artistic. On and on went her talents. It was hard for me not to think that she was simply too good to be true.

The Wranglers told cowboy jokes, they yodeled, they sang 'San Antonio Rose,' 'Cool Water,' 'Red Wing,' and ended up with 'Colorado.' Kate finished the last set with the Wranglers and left the stage followed by appreciative whistles and applause. Stopping for a moment at my table for her guitar case, she touched my arm and said she had to leave to study for an exam or she would stay with me.

'I like you,' she said. 'You take me seriously. Maybe we could meet and I'll see if Sy will join us. Is The Barrel okay? Sometime this week? Say, Tuesday?'

When the singing was finished, Sy sat at a table on stage and was friendly and outgoing, while he sold tapes, 'The Best of the Rocking Bar Wranglers.' After each purchase, he touched the brim of his hat to thank folks for the kind words and support.

That night I couldn't hope to get close to Sy. It seemed

that every member of the audience wanted one of the Wranglers' tapes. So I sat at my picnic table as the crowd surged around the stage.

Rather than trying to horn in on Sy's cassette tape selling, I bought one and at the same time passed him a note explaining that I was a friend of Kate's, as well as Randolph Wells' grandson, and asked if some time he would tell me what he knew of Wells.

Sy opened the note.

'That would be fine,' he said. 'I'd enjoy that, but I'm a little tied up just now.'

He took from his vest a stack of Wranglers business cards, handed one to me, and put the rest on the table by the pile of cassettes.

'Call me in the next day or so,' he said. 'I'm glad you've met my Kate.'

He returned to selling the Wranglers tapes.

Why me? I didn't understand. I was an old forty-five to Kate's energetic nineteen. She must have had her pick of the boys at school. Unless — unless she was attracted to older men who came from Boston, and one in particular who was interested in her and who, more importantly, took her interest seriously.

I could still feel her hand on my arm.

The following afternoon at four-thirty, I had finished half a pitcher of watery Tequila Sunrises before Kate arrived. As she made her way to my table, followed by Ned with a second pitcher, she said hello to almost everyone in the place.

I always did like to watch her move. There was a glow in her cheeks and a swish to her walk that made men look at her.

From what she told me later on, I know that of all the women in Kate's family Carla DuVal, and Carla's mother

May, had the best luck in keeping their men. Although I'm sure Kate realized this, she didn't seem to have any desire to pattern her life after the happy marriages of either her cousin Carla and Ben or after her aunt May and uncle Carl. Perhaps, to her a good marriage was unimaginable. I may well be mistaken in this, but as I look back on it now, it seems possible that she wanted one, one quite possibly with me, but that she didn't know how to go about achieving it.

She settled at my table and Ned removed the pitcher of Sunrises that I was working on, replacing it with a fresh one. She poured herself a glass and began to complain how much school work she wasn't getting done.

'Don't you need an I.D. to drink that?' I asked.

'Ned knows me. Besides, I've got a fake one that says I'm twenty-three.'

'You could pass for that,' I said.

'I know,' she said. 'And don't act like you're my father.'

'Sorry,' I said.

We drank in silence for a time and then I asked her to tell me more about her aunt May. She sparked at that.

'That May was a real prig. And Sy spoiled her,' she said, as I poured another Sunrise from the pitcher. 'I don't understand how Uncle Carl could stand her and Sy's devotion to each other. Of course, I'm sorry she's dead. It hurt Sy terribly — almost as much as when Cassandra died.'

We talked together for an hour, rather she talked about her family and I listened. Then a cowboy swaggered into The Barrel. When she saw him, she picked up her drink.

'I've got to talk to someone,' she said. 'I'll finish about May another time, maybe.'

I watched her sidle over to the guy, who was a good ten years younger than I am. She took off his hat and put it on and slipped her arm around his waist and that,

I thought, was that. So, I moved from our table over to the bar and spent the rest of that dreary night watching her, feeling mighty sorry for myself.

•THREE•

After Kate left The Barrel with the cowboy, I continued to go there almost every afternoon on the off chance that she'd come in. Her friends were there as usual, but without Kate. One afternoon, after a week or so of waiting, I approached a young woman, Sarah McCall, who turned out to be Kate's room-mate, who said she hadn't seen Kate since early that morning — not at lunch or in English. I'd been spending some mornings at the college library searching the archives for Randolph Wells and had not seen Kate there either. She seemed to have turned into a recluse.

On the way back to the Silver Spur I cruised Main, stopping at City Market and Wagon Wheel Liquors. No Kate. After a time, I grew restless in my sterile motel room and went for a walk. A man, middle-aged, graying at the temples, slight build, dressed in khaki shorts and a polo shirt, walked alone, looking for a raven-haired teenager. I passed the fairgrounds and the high school. I crossed the bridge over Junction Creek and sat in the little park, gazing at the water.

In the next few months, I would learn that Kate was by nature a solitary, that she left school some days and was not seen until long after dark and offered no explanation and was vague when pressed. She attended her classes, studied in the library, slept most often in her room at school, but otherwise apparently led a secret, private life off the hill in town. I often saw her walking alone, usually along the Animas River, deep in thought or as if she were searching for someone. She liked to walk, she told me later on, that was all, and look at the people in the cars.

On the evening when I sat in the little park by Junction Creek, I saw her out walking — a kind of dream walking — and had to call out twice before she stopped and turned.

At first she didn't seem to remember me.

'Kate? It's me.'

'Hello.' She seemed sad and preoccupied.

'It's Graden, Kate. Do you want company?'

'Suit yourself. Sure. If you want.'

We left the park and walked north on Main, back the way I'd come. We walked in silence.

Finally, I asked her, 'Who was that guy you left with the other night?'

'What guy?'

'The cowboy.'

'Price. I went out with him a few times earlier in the summer. We broke up.'

'That night I was with you?'

'I guess. Yes. It's made me kind of blue lately.'

'It didn't look that way to me. I mean — he came in and you left like a shot. I thought I'd done something. I didn't know what was wrong.'

'He said he wanted to talk. I'm sorry I was rude. He's married and I didn't know it. I guess his wife found out. Or he told her about us. Anyway, what makes me mad is he lied. He said he wasn't.'

'You like him quite a bit.'

'I did. Not now.'

'How did you meet?'

'I don't remember. It doesn't matter anymore anyway. I probably met him at his laundry. He owns the laundromat out by Trimble Hot Springs. It's near a trailer I have. I take care of a man's horse and use his trailer. He saw me riding and we got to talking. I should have known.'

She gave me a direct, quick look.

'You promise you're not married?'

'Yes. I told you I used to be. A long time ago.'

'Where's your wedding ring?'

'I don't know. I haven't worn it for years.'

'I bet it's in your watch pocket like his was.'

We left Main and went down to the river. By this time we weren't far from my room.

'So, now you're free,' I said, 'of him, at least.'

'I usually am free. I like it that way.'

'Do you want something to eat? I haven't had dinner yet.'

'I would enjoy something hot,' she said. 'Something to make me warm inside.' She smiled at that. A private joke.

We followed the river a distance and came to a small restaurant with outside tables. She ordered a bowl of beef and barley soup.

'This hasn't happened to me before,' she said. 'Usually when I'm out walking no one talks to me. Sure guys yell from cars and honk, but not like this. You picked me up.'

Looking back on what happened, I wonder now as I write this if Kate, behaving like a romantic, did not intentionally imitate the women in her family. By that

I mean, our meeting that afternoon on Main Street definitely has its echo. Her great grandmother Eleanor DuVal was picked up by a man (Joseph Hodges) while she was walking along the Missouri river in St. Charles, as I had picked Kate up. Eleanor eventually married Hodges and he gave her a deadly case of syphilis. When I read Kate's story of Eleanor DuVal — one of many that Kate wrote about her ancestors and kept in a black, three-ring binder — I could not help but suspect, however spontaneous our meeting seemed at the time, that Kate had set it up somehow.

This is what Kate wrote about Eleanor DuVal's first meeting with her future husband, Joseph Hodges:

She was a slight young woman, unlike her mother, and did not have her mother's wild crop of red hair. Yet she did have Helen's way of walking which never failed to catch an eye or cause a man to tip his hat — it's a smooth flowing walk that makes an interesting movement in your hips so your skirt swishes from side to side, revealing a flash of ankle.

My great grandmother would leave the big yellow house on Olive Street in the morning and not be seen until supper was on the table, never volunteering to explain her absence or her whereabouts. She seems to have led a secret life on the other side of town, and the secrets she held within her must have made her feel strong and solitary, making her appear slightly menacing in the eyes of the other young women she knew. Eleanor, the mystery girl, was seen walking alone along the river, as if she were deep in thought or in search of someone. I understand her solitariness — my mother is like that. I am, too, to a certain extent.

'Where do you disappear to?' Eleanor was asked, not a few times. 'Don't you get hungry being gone all day? Who do you speak to? If you have friends you visit, then by all means bring them to the house. I'm glad to have your friends here. I worry about you, Eleanor. I do. One day you might get into trouble and I won't know how to find you.'

'I'm perfectly fine,' she said. 'I like to walk, Mother. That's all. I walk. I think. I look at things and people. It's pleasant. How do you expect me to learn about the world if I coop myself up?' she asked. 'Protect me from what?'

And then during race week, when she was nineteen — my age — and out dream-walking in a daze as usual, she crossed paths with a stranger in the city park, a man who was the opposite of Jacob Stockett, her legal father.

The man walked up to her and asked her name.

'Eleanor,' she said. 'Eleanor DuVal.'

'Are you alone, Miss Eleanor DuVal?'

'Yes. I am always alone,' she said. 'I like it that way.'

'Would you like something to eat? I'll buy you something. Anything you want.' The man was tall. He had a strange sharp-sour smell. She liked his thick, drooping mustache.

'I would enjoy something hot,' Eleanor said. 'Something to make me warm inside.'

'Does your mother know where you are? You do have a mother, don't you?'

'My real mother's dead. Now I have a step-mother, who is also my great aunt.'

The man walked beside Eleanor. His name was Joseph Hodges. She knew he was not from St. Charles. He smelled of camphor and oleander oil. And though it was still March, he was perspiring.

They walked along the river together toward the bridge. He bought her a bowl of oxtail soup. This had

not happened to her before. Usually she met no one.
Time passed so quickly in the company of this man
that she did not realize that she had missed supper
at home. By that time they were far from Olive
Street.

'I've missed supper,' she said. 'I won't make it home
by dark.'

'Don't worry,' he said. 'Let's you and me have
supper together. I'll get you home safely.'

And then it grew dark. She was not afraid of him,
not then. No, she was not afraid, not even when he
took her to his room, not when he removed her
clothes and afterwards let her cover herself with his
robe. It was night by this time and she had forgotten
about going home because she was, in a way, at home
with him. He was polite and, at the same time, gentle
with her. When he made love to her, he was gentle.
He held her and was patient and kind to her as she
expressed her misgivings.

The following morning he walked with her to the
head of her street and said goodbye in a fond way,
and she said that she had enjoyed being with him
and sleeping with him, that it was all so wonderful
and so like a dream and that he was the one whom
she had been looking for on all those days she walked.

Kate out dream-walking along the Animas River, swishing her skirt in that particular way of hers, plays over
and over again in my mind.

Her story of Eleanor continues:

I don't know if it happened to Eleanor, but I do know
that it's happened to my mother, many times. Although it hasn't happened to me yet, I can see
everything that's in the streets, that's in his room —
the chair, the curtains, bureau, narrow bed and all —
and I see the people clearly and hear them. I can
smell him. I know what I have made them say and do

isn't what they really did say and do, but it feels right to me. It's what I would say in the same circumstances and what I would do. So in a way, I am there. Maybe I'm writing more about myself then I am about her.

At home, her parents were frantic with worry. They cried and hugged Eleanor saying that she might have been murdered or kidnapped. Eleanor was, no doubt, impatient and suffered their concern and relief, for she was still lost in her time with Hodges, amazed at how suddenly grown and mature she had become. She was giddy because of her independence, and startled that over one night she had become a woman, finally a woman, with only this slight, annoying soreness between her legs to show for her hours with Hodges.

Eleanor was told to strip and take a bath and was sent immediately afterwards to bed. Her father asked her, severely, to describe the man and to tell him where, not how, but where he had taken her.

She was able to name the rooming house on Water Street by the railroad bridge across town. There her father found the owner, who could identify the man who smelled of camphor and flowers.

'That would be six, Mr. Hodges from Oak Hill, Florida,' said the owner. 'He's here for the races.'

Hodges turned out to be a lumberman who had come to St. Charles looking for customers and a woman, and he had found Eleanor. He told Eleanor's father that he had been misled by her twitching skirt, but, yes, he did bring her to his room anyway, so what, that's what she wanted.

'I didn't use force,' Hodges said. 'None was required.'

Her father, after exerting some pressure, got Hodges to agree not to approach Eleanor again, and if a pregnancy had not resulted from that spontaneous and consenting union between young Eleanor

DuVal and Joseph Hodges, I personally think that man would have been forgotten then and there.

To some extent, my own account of my meeting with Kate is tainted and echoes the Hodges-Eleanor meeting. She finished her beef and barley soup and set the spoon on her napkin. 'This same thing happened to my great grandmother,' Kate said. 'Only she had oxtail soup. They probably don't make it anymore. Who eats oxen these days? Her name was Eleanor and she liked to walk the streets of Saint Charles, the way I do here. She met her husband that way. He turned out to be a very sadistic person.'

'Well, I'm hardly that,' I said.

'And, I bet you don't have syphilis either. Eleanor's husband did. He said that the sores came from being burned by a steam pipe at his lumber mill.'

'Hardly,' I said.

'Eleanor died of it when she was twenty-five,' Kate said off-handedly. 'Her husband also made her get an abortion and she had to bury the fetus in the backyard without a shovel. She used a spoon and her hands to dig the hole.'

'I'm quite clean,' I said, with awkwardness. 'In those areas at least.' Her frank manner disarmed me.

'Isn't it awful?'

'If it's the way you say it is, yes.'

'It is. I've got all the papers to prove it. Do you like to ride horseback? Do you get sore?'

'A little. I haven't tried it in a while.'

'I went yesterday. That horse I take care of is a roan gelding. A beautiful, spirited thing. I'll show him to you if you like. We've got to get some carrots. I like to keep a bag in the barn for him.'

We left the restaurant and walked to the motel to get my car. Joe Aikin's pasture is well north of town in the river valley. We drove on to the place and Kate introduced me to the horse, a frisky reddish horse called Flame. Near the barn was the small faded yellow trailer.

I live here now, where she once lived, beside the Animas River — the river of lost souls.

When Kate lived here, the place was bright and clean inside and she had it decorated with flower print curtains and colorful braided rugs. All of that is still here. But it's never been as bright again. This was her hideaway from school. She came here to study and to sleep. She brought her lover, the cowboy-laundryman, here. She brought me.

Our time passed quickly that evening. She had missed dinner at school. Soon it was dark. She did not want to go and did not want me to leave her. She said nothing of the laundryman and asked me to open her blouse and to hold her. She pressed herself close against me and with a calm and matter of fact expression asked me if I would like to make love with her.

Kate was not calculating — far from that — she was business-like and certain. Afterwards she asked me to get her robe and she wrapped herself in it and turned her back to me to sleep.

At all times, even during our first act of love, I was gentle with her, perhaps too gentle and not passionate enough. When she opened her legs and pulled me to her, I was slightly hesitant and careful. I held her and was controlled and remained kind and considerate to her at all times — even during the heat of our passion — and I did not express doubts or reservations. She was, after all, nineteen years old and I was forty-five. This seemed to make no difference to her.

'You don't have to be so gentle,' she said. 'I can take it.'

So I was less so.

I stayed with her all that night and drove her up the hill to school the next morning before breakfast, leaving her outside the cafeteria. As she crossed the parking lot, I watched her walk. Her way of walking made me want her again. I was not concerned by how young she was — not now. She had what I came to call 'Eleanor's walk,' a smooth, flowing stride that gave a sensual movement to her hips and made her short skirt swish from side to side, revealing a flash of her thigh. Her body came alive as she walked, and I now knew that body and the captivating movement of her hips. I was besotted by her even then.

We went to her trailer in Aikin's pasture often after that. Usually we'd meet at The Barrel and drink for a while and then we'd stop for something to eat and come here, most often for the night if she had no morning class.

As I mentioned earlier, this is my trailer now. I'm renting it from Joe Aikin and look after his horse Flame. I use her chair and her bureau and her narrow bed and I open her flower print curtains to look out on the pasture, once green with alfalfa, now hidden with snow. And I smell her still when I bury my face in her pillow or wrap myself up in her terrycloth robe and try to sleep.

•Four•

Kate and I had been lovers for three or four weeks when one afternoon she did not meet me at The Barrel as arranged. So I went out to her trailer uninvited. I thought she might be sick. She had not missed a rendezvous before and I was worried. It's my right, I thought, it's a lover's right to worry and to inquire.

It was just after eight, a beautiful late summer night, and her lights were on. The crickets sounded in Aikin's pasture and Flame, who saw me drive across the pasture, stopped nuzzling grass to lift his wild head in brief greeting.

Kate must have seen my car lights, for when I rapped loudly, heartily on the screen she immediately opened the door a crack. But, she did not unlock the screen. I pulled on it. I rattled it.

'What are you doing here?' she said, irritated. 'Did I

invite you? Did I ask you to come and check on me? Nobody's supposed to come here unless they're invited by me. Not even you, Graden.'

She wore her/my pale terrycloth robe. Her hair was up. At first, I thought someone, her cowboy-laundry-man, was in there with her.

'I looked for you at The Barrel. I thought we were going to meet.'

'I decided I didn't want to.'

'You decided? So, how was I supposed to know that? Should I leave? Do you want me to go, is that it?'

'No. But don't come out here looking for me. I hate that. I really hate it. This is my private place.' She unlocked the screen. 'As long as you understand that, you can come on in just this once.'

Though I'd been there many times before and regularly slept with her in her bed, that night I entered the trailer as an unwelcome stranger. I had unknowingly crossed a line which had made her angry at me; I had committed a breach of conduct.

'What's wrong?' I asked. 'I don't understand you sometimes. Why are you so angry?'

'John Pratt used to do that very same thing to my grandmother Cassandra,' she said, as if that explained it all — her irritation, her coldness. 'He ran a turpentine camp in Georgia. Sit. Go ahead, sit down. I'm sorry I was rude. I'll get you a beer if you want one.'

We drifted for a while in small talk. Finally, she took my hand.

'Anyway,' she said, 'here's the way it goes for my grandmother over and over. Year after year. When the rainy season begins, Pratt closes his camp and goes to Cassandra. She never knows beforehand when he's coming. He just shows up the way you did. She's all calm and occupied, maybe reading to her little girls, my mother and my aunt May, and he bangs on her screen door, and Cassandra drops everything. Her world stops. He becomes suddenly the center of attention. Nothing else matters. She forgets about everything but him.

'Mother said it was awful when Pratt arrived. He didn't like Cassandra's girls much. But Cassandra worshiped him. Pratt was king of the house for a month. Then as suddenly as he came, he went away and they had to pick up their lives where they left off, until the next time.

'No man is ever going to do that to me, not any man ever again. I can't stand to be surprised and swept away. Cassandra would do whatever Pratt wanted — any time, any place. She was too blind to see the fool he made of her, but the girls weren't. Mother said Cassandra could be washing dishes and she'd leave them when the knock came, leave them mid-dish. And they'd stay like that, cold in the sink, until Pratt left.'

'She must have loved him,' I said, hopefully.

'She loved him too much, if you ask me. She should have loved Sy like that. He's worth it. Besides, Graden, that guy Price Jones used to surprise me, just like Pratt did Cassandra. He'd close the laundromat and come over here whenever he felt like it. And like a fool I let him in. I won't go through that again. I'm not always in the mood, sometimes I want to be alone. That's the way it is. I am not at anyone's beck and call.'

'I understand that, Kate. Tell me. What were you doing when I knocked on your screen and you thought I was John Pratt?'

'Washing the dishes.'

'Let's finish them, shall we, before the water gets cold.'

'It doesn't matter. It's just a frying pan and some silverware. Let them soak.'

She had quieted down some. She touched my cheek.

'I like you, Graden. I really do. But please don't do that again.'

We stood elbow to elbow at her little sink. The window was open and the breeze off the river carried the smell of freshly cut alfalfa.

'Tell me about your parents, will you?' I asked, 'You hardly mention them. Is your father still alive?'

'Mother lives in Santa Fe. You'll meet her. I think she's coming up for Parents' Weekend. I don't know who my father is. She doesn't know, either.'

'Where he is, you mean?'

'Well, that and *who* he is, really.'

I dried the frying pan and set it on the two-burner, counter-top cooker.

'To begin with, Eva — my mother — raised me the way she was raised, without a father. Eva's real father was Cassandra's half brother Elliot, but that wasn't spoken of. John Pratt, Cassandra's husband, was Aunt May's father. So, when my mom grew up, her sister May had Pratt for a father — for what that was worth — but Mom didn't have anyone who would claim her as his daughter. Cassandra's brother Elliot wouldn't own up to her; and Pratt, even though Mom wanted Pratt as her father, the way he was her sister May's father, he would have nothing to do with her — at least not then. Later, he had a lot to do with her, the bastard.

'Mom as a kid was put at arm's length by the two important men in her childhood — Elliot and Pratt. That made her a loner, I think. And I, too, grew up with no important men in my life. There wasn't ever a regular, steady man at Eva's because the men just came and then left. Because of this, at home, people sort of shy away from us. We're not unfriendly or anything, we just keep to ourselves. Eva has her name on the mailbox. She gets her propane tank filled and her kerosene delivered and has her charge accounts at the grocery and the hardware store and keeps up her shares on the ditch above her place. But, essentially, she's a solitary.

'And she's lived that way since I was born, rooted in that same valley on that same thirty acres north of Santa Fe in that same adobe house, always with her fruit trees, her goats, a garden and a black-and-white border collie called Peter. She's not worried about the rest of the world. She never has been. As for me, I was sent off to school. I've been away from home at school since I was twelve. Sometimes I think I was raised by schools. I don't see Mom except on vacations. And I've never met my father. Don't you think it's strange? She didn't care enough about him even to find out who he was.'

Kate and I left the kitchen and sat down together on her bed.

'Mother won't commit herself to any man,' Kate said. 'She's afraid to, is what I think. They get close to her and she shuts them out. I don't want to be like her. I hope I don't turn out that way.'

'Why is she afraid?'

'I think it's because of what Pratt did to Cassandra. He controlled my grandmother. Like I said, she'd drop everything to be with him. And he didn't love her, not the way Sy did, does. To Pratt, my grandmother was just another woman who was available for him.'

'How do you know that?'

'Mom told me. She also told me that when she was my age, after Cassandra died, that she was Pratt's lover for a while. I know you probably think that's sick, but she was. She wanted him to like her, to accept her, and thought that was the way to do it. After that she had a string of men. And one of them is my father. It's the way Mom is. I'm used to it, I guess. She's always had someone different living with her for a while. So my father is just some man she met. She doesn't know where he is.'

'She never saw him again?'

'Right. He was just passing through. It was like that. Very casual. She has men like that. I'm used to it. She's my mother, after all, not some whore. And she isn't a whore. Every now and then she wants a man, so she finds herself one. But I'm not like that.'

'What do you want, Kate?'

'A man, eventually. A life. One good man, one good life.'

'Like your grandmother?'

'Yes. Except she picked the wrong one. She should have picked Sy Cooke.'

'You think of lot of Sy.'

'He's way too old for me, if that's what you mean. Besides, he's still in love with her.'

All these people were so clear to Kate. And the more she told me about them, the clearer they were becoming to me.

'Where do you think Eva met your father?' I asked.

'If he's the one I think he is, they met at a Pic N' Save in Bernalillo. And he must have been nice. He probably carried her things to her car for her and then helped her unload them at home. Besides, she wanted a baby. That's what she told me. She picked this guy to be the father.

'There were a few other men around her at the same time as the Pic N' Save guy.'

She went to the small dining table and brought me her black, three-ring binder which holds Kate's stories of the DuVal women. I have it here with me as I write.

Eva DuVal's story is first and in it is a list of five men, all of whom Eva knew in 1969. Any one of them could be Kate's dad.

She describes her potential fathers like this:

1) Wyatt Jones — He was a stock car racer from Albuquerque. Mother might still be with him if he had given up racing or if she had become used to the races — the dirt, the noise, the exhaust, the outfits she was expected to wear just to get in the winner's photograph in the *Journal* to satisfy the sponsors. She liked the thrill at first. But then his accident made her freeze tight and become rigid. She could not put on her silver bathing suit or sit on the fender and would not allow champagne to be poured be-

tween her breasts, not after Wyatt Jones's accident. So they broke up.

2) Arnold Fosnot — He did soul-work on my mother, as Jones did body-work. She said she went out with him because he woke her up, woke up her spirit and inner being. She went to California with him and was there for a month or so. Fosnot gave seminars on healing. Mother wore tight turquoise slacks and flimsy sandals and did his promotion work. They lived in motels. Mother asked him to give her a reading.

'We were driving on U.S. One, north of Big Sur, on our way to San Francisco,' she said. 'He told me that I made such bad choices in men because I took them all from the same soul group as my father. "Which father?" I asked, laughing at him. He said I would not succeed in breaking the pattern of picking men who were not good for me. "Does this include you?" I asked him. "Yes. I'm afraid it does," he said. So I left him in San Jose.'

3) Robert Clark — She met him in San Francisco. He lived on a boat near Fisherman's Wharf. She was working as a dancer on the hill and often went home with men like him. Clark took her to his boat. Later, Mother escaped to the main deck and dove over the side. She left her clothes, along with her purse and necklace and watch and keys on a table and dove into the bay in her bra and panties. They told her later, when she was registered as a Jane Doe in the hospital, that she was found washed up near Fisherman's Wharf. They thought she had tried to kill herself. She probably did.

4) Sean Delaney — He is a psychologist she met in Taos in the summer of 1969. She called him a 'clinical' person. He told her that we marry those who are like our mothers, men and women alike, not our fathers. He was a vague, fragile man who cried when they made love the first time. He was too gentle and

he lacked abandon and passion and humor. But, he cared for her and cared for her and cared for her. He was, if anything, the opposite of her mother Cassandra — a man without a center, a man who cared more about healing Mom than he did about loving her for herself. He wanted her to remain his dear, perennial patient, always getting better, always better, but never well.

When Mother saw this man again three summers ago, he was with his twin sons, in a stroller, and a pregnant wife. Mother said she quickly turned and bent toward a Navajo woman selling pawn jewelry from a blanket. She came away with the squash blossom and turquoise necklace. (I love that necklace. She gave it to me when I left home for college. I wear it all the time.) Seeing Sean Delaney again made her sad and confused, it made her almost wish she could have been his wife, wish she could have had all that — the twins and the successful husband. If she had that, she thought, then maybe she would be almost happy and her life would have some deeper meaning. Mother was not certain. She gets sad that way sometimes. She still isn't sure if she should have left Sean Delaney.

5) The Pic N' Save Man — She brought him home from shopping. He carried her new toaster oven and her new blender into the house and he stayed for a few days, but Eva doesn't know his name or how to find him. She doesn't remember anything more about him. Or she won't say. He's the mystery man and I think the love of her life to whom she was afraid to commit herself.

I read the list and closed Kate's notebook, which she took from me and carefully put on her bookshelf.

'So, Graden, any one of them could be my father,' she said. 'The timing's right. I can pick the one I want. When I was a kid, I liked the race car guy, and later on the shrink, Sean Delaney. That preacher, I always thought, was a real jerk-off and so was that rich guy in San Francisco, but on top of that he was also a cruel, rich bastard.

'I vote for the Pic N' Save guy. I'm thinking now that he's the one. But it doesn't really matter because I'll never know for sure.

'Mom's different. She goes for serial lovers, what I call faceless men. She has them one after the other and doesn't want to know anything about them. One left her pregnant with me. The faceless ones, she thinks they're better than that shadow, that tyrant John Pratt, who Cassandra waited for. She likes a string of men and not that single waited-for one who raps on the screen, the one who demolishes the world when the door is opened for him.'

We were lying side by side now.

Kate faced the ceiling. Her soft, fragrant robe had come open and I was slowly moving my palm over her nipples, just touching them.

'You're not like any of them,' she said. 'So, don't worry. Also, Graden, you aren't my father substitute. You aren't even like anybody on that list.'

'I'm glad of that.'

'So am I,' she said, kissing me. 'Why don't you at least take off your shoes. Now that you're here — uninvited — you might as well stay.'

•Five•

I tried to respect Kate's wishes and stayed away from her trailer, unless invited there, relying on meeting her at The Barrel when she wanted to be with me; so I was pleasantly surprised when, a few days later, Kate woke me at the Silver Spur to say she had an exam first period, but the rest of the morning was free. If she could get some horses and a truck and trailer from her uncle Carl, would I like to ride up to the lake and see my grandfather's place?

I picked her up an hour later at school and we drove north out of the valley. Carl Haffey's packing and trail riding business was just beyond the entrance to Haviland Lake. He was off on a hour's ride with a group of greenhorns and one of his hands had the trailer hitched when we got there. He and Kate got our two horses from the corral and loaded them into the trailer. She picked her childhood horse, Blue Belle, and gave me Peanuts to ride.

At Purgatory Campgrounds, she got the horses out of the trailer. They were saddled and content, nibbling oats from their feed bags. It was about ten thirty, and the sun was just rising off the cliffs and it promised to be positively hot. I had not been astride a horse for nearly twenty years, if not more, but soon we were on a gentle bluff; not far below us was the old Silverton-Durango stagecoach road.

As we rode through the woods, Kate explained that Aunt May was nineteen and working as a breakfast waitress in the Slickrock (Colorado) Cafe when she met Carl Haffey, in 1959. He was a hunting and fishing guide who ran a string of pack horses out of Ophir into the Uncompahgres. After they married, May quit her job and moved into his cabin near Trout Lake where Kate's cousin Carla was born six months later.

Kate said that Carl and May Haffey always had horses, too many horses to feed some winters when business was slow. But for all their married life, no matter how hard the times, they never even came close to starving to death. They made do. Lived poor sometimes, feeding the animals before themselves when it came to it. Accepted only what they needed from Cassandra, though she offered two, three times more than that.

When May's share of Cassandra's estate passed on to her, she used it to buy the land and buildings on their spread north of town. Carl Haffey's pack horse business became stable then, cushioned by Cassandra's money in slow times when it was too cold or the ground was too snow-covered to venture into the mountains.

As a young girl, Carla was forever helping her father take care of the horses or repairing tack or packing gear for one of his trips, and when she was twelve she was allowed to take small parties on day trips up Lizardhead Pass to fish and picnic.

'My cousin is a natural on a horse,' said Kate. 'I always wanted to ride as well as she does. As girls we used to strip and take my Blue Belle and her Tess into Trout Lake near the house. Later, when Carla was about eighteen and I was just barely nine, she taught me — dared me, really — to dive from Blue Belle's back. I can still remember how Carla's thin white body arched before it cut into the clear waters and how she came up sputtering, grabbing for my ankle, screaming for me to pull her up from the cold. And then I dove and Carla pulled me up, this tall skinny kid, shivering and proud, onto Tess's back, up in front of her.

'When Carla was in high school, she practically ran the business for her father. May was sick then, but they didn't know what was wrong — weak, sleepy, no energy. Then I think Carla got fed up, taking care of everything. When she graduated from high school, she left home with her first husband. She was in Wyoming when Aunt May was diagnosed with liver cancer. Then she was in New York City with her second husband when her mother died four years ago. Liver cancer, the same thing Grandmother Cassandra died from.

'When May died, Sy had his first stroke. Carla has always said it was her mother's cancer death and not Sy's hard life catching up with his heart that threw him down on the boards one night in the middle of an after-dinner show at Fort Wilderness, his fiddle flung across the stage. At first Carla looked after Sy, but she couldn't manage him, the swim shop and the pack business. So Sy sent for his grandson Ben.'

We rode on through the aspen and sloping mountain meadows.

'Why are you so interested in your grandfather?' she asked. 'I always thought he was just some Eastern asshole with a lot of someone else's money to throw around. No offence.'

'He was that,' I said. 'But, if you consider that at least he had the reputation for being friendly and not snobbish, as you'd expect of an Easterner, then it's possible that he liked the country and was not just a playboy in a gold camp. What interests me is what drove him. What made him marry the daughter of a boarding-house owner rather than the rich socialite? He married a rich woman the first time, a Wentworth. Why not again? Also I want to know why he built the cabin. What did he want it for? He may have been a hermit, after all, not the well-connected playboy. Perhaps, he was gradually moving deeper and deeper into isolation and solitude.

'You see, Kate, my grandfather had no profession, no trade, no financial resources, except for what he charmed away from the Eastern families he met at Harvard. At the sign of a recession in the early twenties, these people pulled their money out of high risk mineral exploration. That left him out in the cold.'

'Didn't he kill himself up here?' she asked. 'That's what I've always heard.'

The old stagecoach road runs parallel with U.S. 550, so we dropped off the bluff and cut through the pines and bush-whacked due east for a mile or so to the old road and then headed south toward the north end of Electra Lake. On the way in, we followed the easement over Forest Service land and came across the fresh-cut stakes with orange surveyor's tape tied to them, marking off the future road that would be cut if I were to sell the place. Kate noticed the survey was recent. I offered her no explanation, at least not then. When we crossed onto my property, I was surprised by the surge of ownership that came over me.

This was the first land of any real value I had owned — not counting the few lots I had in Ipswich which I gave to my ex-wife in the property settlement years earlier. My mother had a summer house and a few acres in Seabrook, New Hampshire, which I sold to KOA for a campground after she died. Those parcels were nothing compared with fifty-plus acres of virgin land at the edge of a private lake in the Southern Rockies. The survey has the plot shaped like a trapezoid with the wide side on the shore front and the narrow up at the head of a gorge. The land drops maybe a hundred feet in half a mile from red cliffs to wetlands. The old stagecoach road cuts through the western corner and there are at least ten or twelve wonderful building sites with a view of the lake and the West Needles and the Animas valley to the south. The property on each side is Forest Service. It would be easy to cut a road — a switch back through the woods — and to tie it into the old stagecoach road.

Here were rock cliffs and aspen groves, meadows and ridges. The sun made the pine needles smell sweet and strong. About seventy thousand dollars would clear the building sites and another one hundred or a hundred-and-a-half would cut the road. I could have sold off all but five acres around my grandfather's place and made myself a bundle.

We rode along the western boundary line down to the lake and then followed the shore to the eastern line — a distance of almost five hundred yards. Canada geese were grumbling as they fed in the grass a distance away and were not bothered by our horses.

'Somebody's spent a ton of money on this survey,' Kate said. 'Stakes every twenty-five feet at least.'

She brought Blue Belle close to one of them and leaned onto the horse's neck intending to pull the stake.

'Please leave it there,' I said. 'It's my survey.'

'Why? Are you going to sell?'

'I have it on the market.'

'Graden! You can't do that. Someone will come in here and build houses. The place will be destroyed. I ride up here all the time. Uncle Carl hunts up here. Carla and I used to take Sy's boat and camp out at the old cabin. You can't do it.'

'What else is there to do with it?'

'Nothing. Pretend it isn't yours. Just leave it. Come on, let me show you something.'

I followed her away from the lake shore on a cow trail. We topped a rock knoll and the lake was suddenly below us. Overlooking the clear dark water, a short distance away from us, was my grandfather's cabin, what was left of it.

'See? Who else in the world owns a setting like this. I love it here. Don't sell. Please don't.'

Electra Lake is formed by a timber-crib-and-rock-filled dam which stops the flow of Elbert Creek. It's almost three miles long, filling what was once a deep valley. The valley's cliffs, Bishop Pond and a section of the old stagecoach road are now hidden by the lake's dark, black water. At the far end, where Kate and I were, are meadows and aspen groves protected on both sides by high mountains — Engineer, Spud, and the Twilights. In the center of the lake is Big Island. On the west side, south of Big Island a few hundred yards, is Vail Point, where Sy Cooke's cabin sits on a low peninsula rich with tall, thick-barked ponderosa pines, quaking aspen, wild roses and scrub oak.

My grandfather's cabin was there before the valley was flooded, before Vail Point was transformed by rising water from a promontory in the cliffs into a peninsula. Cabins lower than his were either abandoned or dismantled by their owners and moved to higher ground. Thirty or so were eventually set in the trees around the southern end by the dam. Summer cabins. Those abandoned are visible at times below the lake's surface. If the light slants at a certain angle and the surface is smooth, one can pick out metal roofs, stumps, window holes and the skeletons of drowned pines, all hanging in suspension twenty or thirty feet below — the remains of a small scattered village under permanent deluge. From time to time a plank or a shutter will surface, but for the most part the cabins and sheds and trees stand quiet in the dark, cold lake waters.

We made our way to the cabin itself.

'Keep your reins loose,' said Kate. 'Peanuts can find his own way down. Tell me how your grandfather died.'

'I know two versions,' I said. 'In the first; he borrows twenty dollars from a friend to buy a gun to shoot himself, because he doesn't want to pawn any of the memorabilia he has collected out here in the West to pay for the gun.

'In the second; he borrows a hundred dollars from a friend and puts it in his pocket before he jumps over the side of his row boat with rocks tied around his ankles, so he doesn't die broke.

'In either case, his influence was nil by that time and his charm, at least according to my father, was stripped away just as sure as if it had been blown off his head like a top hat in a wind storm. Still his suicide confuses me, even though it's somehow fitting, an inevitable conclusion.'

'You don't like him that much, do you?'

'Well, that's not the point. He killed himself. I wish I'd known him.'

The last fifty yards were blocked by a fall of aspen and a beaver pond. We tied the horses and scrambled over the dead trees and crossed the mud and twig dam in front of the abandoned cabin. The place was no less rugged than Sy's cabin and is not difficult to get to by boat, or even for a greenhorn on an old horse.

'As girls, Carla and I packed in here once for three days,' said Kate.

The cabin is one room with a fireplace, outhouse, well, and tool shed. The privy is a two-holer that hangs over the stream and is swept clean each year in the spring run-off.

Before I saw the place I wondered why a man at the peak of his influence, with rich friends and a generous patron, would drop out like he did to live there. Yet, in my grandfather's time, as now, some college kids came West in the summer. They drank and played around. Some dropped out and stayed. But Grandfather was not such a personality. He glad-handed the miners. He speculated. Why did he need that cabin? Was he broke and in retreat? How could a man who lived on $75,000 a year survive in such isolation, a man who had been called 'the owner of Telluride' let himself be reduced to this? Why a two-hole privy? Did he have a companion? If so, who? So much I didn't know.

The cabin had been abused over the years by hunters, but was still in fair shape; it could be made livable. There was an ample supply of wood and the well had water but needed cleaning.

'If I were to live up here, perhaps you'd pack in supplies,' I said.

'Or Uncle Carl will. It's his business,' she said. 'Don't you just love it up here? I don't see how you can even think of selling it.'

The woodstove was too far gone to salvage. But there was a fireplace. Someone — Kate or Carl — would check on me now and again. I could move out if the winter became too severe. The roof was rotten tin over sawn heart pine boards that were in good shape.

Kate went past the well toward the privy. Down the hill, on the stream side of the knoll, she found the small tool shed. Nothing inside had been touched for years. The saw and axe, hatchet, sledge, wedges, crowbar were all still coated with a thin film of grease.

'I wouldn't mind living here,' I said, but she had not heard me.

After perhaps an hour of exploring, Kate and the horses became restless. On the way out, Peanuts and Blue Belle covered the ground quickly, eager to get home—across the gorge to the stagecoach road, up to the bluff and on through the pines to U.S. 550 and the campground—a forty-five-minute ride each way.

We walked the horses a while to let them cool down before loading them back into the trailer.

'So you live in Boston?' she asked.

'I did, outside of Boston in Concord. I worked for a brokerage firm in town. But I don't know if I'll go back. I've done it since I was twenty-five. That seems long enough. I'm tempted just to walk away from it and live in the mountains by myself.'

'It can get real boring alone,' said Kate. 'You'd be surprised how fast you run out of stuff to think about. I like having a place where I go to be alone. But a day or two is enough. If you lived back there at your grandfather's place, I bet you'd last a week. Do you have kids?'

'No kids. We waited too long, I guess. Or we never wanted any.'

'I thought so,' she said. 'And you can just quit your job?'

'I have enough to live on, if I'm reasonably careful.'

'If I had lots of money I'd travel all the time. I'd go places to learn more about my family. I've done it some, but not enough. Did your family move around?'

'My mother's family stayed in New England, but my father's got spread out. Dad was seven when Grandfather Randolph killed himself. He left Telluride and went back east to school. He met my mother in Boston. When she died, he went back home to work at the Tomboy Mine out of Telluride as an engineer and then he got a job in Albuquerque, where he was caught up in the uranium boom, lost some money, and then he worked for a few oil companies. He died just a few months ago.'

'Oh, I'm sorry. How did it happen?'

'A car accident. He just ran off the road near Santa Fe.'

'You sound like you think he did it on purpose?'

'He was a careful driver. He just didn't make a turn in a road he drove all the time. Maybe it was on purpose. I don't know. After all, his dad killed himself.'

'Sometimes you don't know. Or there's no explaining it. It seems like the next step to take. The next logical step. My great grandmother, Eleanor, was very sick before she died. I think she let herself go. She did it with rat poison because she had syphilis. That's what I think I would do. If it came to it. My life. I mean, it's possible. But, not with rat poison.'

'I hope you don't. Why would you?'

'Who can say? I'd have to have a really good reason,' she said.

We were silent for a time, leading the horses up and down the edge of the highway, cooling them down. Kate was like Eleanor DuVal, I suppose. At least, she walked the way Eleanor did, with that swishing of her hips, a swing from side to side that must have been practiced. A sensual, rolling walk. I have no idea, of course, if Eleanor could ride as well as Kate. Flirtatious Kate.

'Anyway, I think I met your grandmother a few times,' she said. 'When I went to Telluride with Carla and Sy.'

'You couldn't have known Mattie Wells, Kate. She died in nineteen fifty six, years before you were born.'

'Mattie Wells's candy store. Is it the one on Main by the court house?'

'That's the one. The original sign is still there.'

'Well, I've been in it. Sy and Cassandra always took us there for pralines. It was kind of a tradition. I liked to visit Grandmother Cassandra. We fished and went on picnics. And we always went to the candy store for pralines.'

'It's owned by a couple of women now. They haven't changed the name. They got a kick out of meeting the founder's grandson.'

We got the horses in the trailer. She secured the door.

'Have you always lived in the east?' Kate asked.

'Mother died when I was at Andover. So I stayed in school out there and went on to Yale. Then I was offered a job in Boston.'

'And now you're here. I hope you decide to stay.'

It was almost one o'clock when we got back to town, and Kate declined lunch.

'I bet I get saddle sores,' I said. 'Thanks for the ride anyway.'

'You did okay for a greenhorn.'

'And you look perfect on a horse, like you were born on one. Why don't we do this more often?'

'We just might,' she said. 'Anyway, I'll see you.'

'You'll be in The Barrel later?'

'Maybe,' she said, giving me her blank stare.

'Well, I'll look for you then. Maybe you'll change your mind.'

•Six•

When I called Sy Cooke to arrange for the interview he'd promised, he immediately invited me up to his cabin on Vail Point the next evening, when the Wranglers had no performance. I arrived about five-thirty. It was a Tuesday in early September and the aspen had turned, covering the Point and the surrounding hillsides with a blaze of color.

Sy's log cabin was built by the power company in 1906. It was a single room then, like my grandfather's, and used as a dam construction office by P.C. Schools, the manager. Sy Cooke worked for P.C. as a kid and finally bought the place from him in 1941, when Carla's and Kate's grandmother moved from Telluride to Denver.

When Ben married Carla in 1985, he added the kitchen and first floor bedroom and the stairs to their room, replacing the attic ladder. And he put in the picture window and the cut stone fireplace. The ceiling light fixture was made by Joe Aikin. The horseshoes around the sockets were a gift to Sy from the girls' grandmother Cassandra. They came off her horse Buttons. Both Kate and Carla rode that horse as children.

Carla and Ben have no children yet. She is twenty-eight and looks maternal with her short, stocky build. She has a full, white face with pink-tinged cheeks and small, dark eyes. A solid woman with a low center of gravity. The afternoon that I met her she wore a man's shirt, open at the collar, showing a mass of freckles above her full bosom.

When I arrived there, none of us realized that Kate had not been seen at school for almost twenty-four hours. She had not returned to campus from town the night before. Though she was expected for supper that evening, she had not called to confirm.

Kate had not met me in The Barrel the night before. I spent a good three hours there waiting for her. I don't know if she was with someone else.

'I saw her last week,' I said. 'We took a ride to my grandfather's cabin. I haven't seen her since.'

I didn't want them to notice how much Kate's absence disappointed me.

After getting me a drink, Carla excused herself to call her cousin's dormitory. There was a coldness about Carla, and I thought that Kate had probably told her about me and that she didn't approve.

Sarah McCall, Kate's roommate, answered the phone and told Carla only that Kate was not there. She did not say that Kate had not returned to their room the previous night 'simply because at the time no one was worried about her, and besides,' Sarah said to me later on, 'her social life isn't any of Carla's business.'

'I'll try again later,' Carla said and hung up.

Sy, who had been reading a western in front of the

cabin's woodstove, offered a chair across the stove from him.

'It's not like her,' Carla said. 'I told her you might be here. Usually she calls to cancel. It's not like her not to let us know.'

Sy shrugged as if to say: 'Let's get over this little mix-up straight away, then we'll be in business.' He was clearly anticipating being interviewed and not worried in the least about Kate.

'She's not coming,' he said. 'It's happened before.'

'Something better came up,' said Ben.

Ben Cooke is thirty and is not much taller than his wife. His face is hidden by a full beard, making him seem bearish. He wears wire-framed glasses for reading and his shirt hints at rolls of fat around his mid-section. He and his wife both have dark hair, not as black as Kate's. Ben's eyes are hazel, but sometimes look dark green.

We sipped our drinks and waited. It was obvious that Kate was not going to arrive.

The three occupants of the cabin look alike in a certain way, as people who live in close quarters sometimes do, except Sy has a world-weary manner and is more open and friendly. I had no reason to feel any special affinity toward Ben and Carla, a somewhat off-putting young couple, and was concerned that Carla's continued worry about Kate would inhibit my talk with Sy.

Ben was occupied grading papers at the table in the cabin's main room. Among the papers was Kate's latest installment of her family's history, each of which she turned in to Ben's composition class.

'Maybe she's on her way here now and didn't stop off at school,' Carla said. 'I might as well put in the roast. We should leave you alone for your interview, shouldn't we, Sy?'

'Why don't I treat us to supper?' Ben said. 'We'll drive up to Lime Creek for steaks.'

'You buying?' asked Sy.

'I'm worried about her,' Carla said. 'We should be here if she comes.'

'She won't come,' said Ben. 'What's there to worry about? Probably she met someone last night and has forgotten all about us. We'll hear from her when she remembers. Don't forget she's my student. She's the type who gets side-tracked. Half the time she doesn't hand in her work. Why should she eat with us, her own family, when she's found someone more exciting?'

Carla went across the room from the telephone to the table where her husband was working. She kissed him on the back of his neck.

'Let's go upstairs and leave them alone,' she said.

'That would be appreciated,' said Sy. And after they'd gone, he said, 'Now then, Randolph Wells. I knew him, of course. I also knew a woman named Wells in Telluride, Mattie Wells. Did you ever hear of her? A tall skinny woman.'

'She was my grandmother.'

'Your grandmother?' he said. 'I knew her first as Mattie McBride. I think her father ran a boarding house.'

'That was before she married my grandfather.'

'Didn't she run the telegraph office and candy store?'

'That's right. It's next to the court house in a brick building on the up-hill side of Main Street. When I was there in July to bury my father, I found her grave marker. The boarding house has been torn down.'

'I don't know how many times I took Cassandra's girls to Mattie's Candy Store when I was up visiting Cassandra. First Eva and May and then the grand-daughters.'

'You knew her?'

'Well, I knew who she was. She always had a supply of pralines for the girls.'

'She died in nineteen fifty-six when I was eighteen. I hadn't been West yet and was still in school. My dad went out to see her a few times when I was little. But

Mattie never came East to visit my mother or me.'

'Mattie Wells was Randolph's wife? I never knew she had a husband.'

'She was only married to him for a few years — ten or so — before he left her to move down here. She didn't move with him. I'm not sure why. My father was her only child, as far as I know.'

'Well, I knew her to speak to.'

'I wish I had, of course.'

Sy leaned back in his chair, savoring, no doubt, the memory of his visits to Telluride to visit Cassandra.

'So you're Mattie Wells's grandson? Damn, I guess that makes us practically family. I'm afraid that I knew her slightly better than I did your grandfather, which isn't saying that much. Why don't you give me a run-down on what you've learned so far, and I'll try and fill you in.'

I told Sy that my grandfather came to Colorado from New York City during the gold and silver boom of the late 1890s and early 1900s. He was financed by Harry Payne Whitney, at the insistence of Whitney's wife Louise, who gave Grandfather between eight and eleven million dollars over a fifteen-year period to operate Telluride's Smuggler Union Mining Company, of which he was president and general manager. From what I've learned, he was known as a womanizer, a dabbler, a taste-maker, a fast talker, a man who relied on the Whitney fortune, as meted out by Louise. He charged the Whitneys $75,000 for personal expenses alone in 1921, the year Louise cut him off — because he did not marry her Denver friend Alice Crawford Hill, a recent widow. He married Mattie McBride, the town's telegraph operator, instead. Grandfather was Louise Whitney's vicarious presence on the frontier, and he answered to her for successful or failed ventures. It was Louise, not Harry, whom he wired when a half-million dollar settlement over claim jumping came down on their side in the circuit court at Telluride, and it was

Louise who through spite cut off his money flow in 1922. Before that he traveled widely — to Mexico, China, California, Nevada, France — relying on charm and the belief in charm's power to support him, which it did until his balloon burst. Then down he came, empty, and without the respect he formerly held. The bottom dropped out of his life the moment the Whitney money stopped. Shortly after Grandfather's fall from grace, he moved to his cabin.

'I know that he contracted the job through Jackson Hardware of Durango,' said Sy. 'I worked for them back then. His cabin's at the north end of the lake, back in the woods two miles from here. I haven't been up there for years.'

'I've seen it,' I said, 'with Kate.'

'I built that place for him in nineteen six. That grandfather of yours didn't know which end of a hammer was up. He was no more than a big dandy of a fish in that little pond,' said Sy. 'Let me tell you a curious fact about Wells. His handshake was firm, but his fingers and palm were soft, like a woman's. I remember that best about him. I was just a kid and he bent down and looked me in the eye. He towered above me. His hat was a big white cloud. He reached down and took my hand in his. It was soft. I won't forget how smooth and soft that hand was. It did not belong in this country. It was not the hand of a man who worked for a living. I was shocked by how soft it was.'

Sy didn't say whether it was good or bad to work for Randolph Wells.

'He was a dilettante type. His silver tongue and his charm did his work for him, whatever that work was, not his skill or his hands.'

With still no word from Kate, Sy interrupted the interview and we all drove in the Cookes' van up Coal Bank Hill to the Lime Creek Lodge for beer and steaks grilled blood-red.

Afterwards Ben resumed grading papers. Carla arranged the fall grasses she had collected earlier in the day onto the pages of her flower press. She wondered out loud if she should call to see if Kate was all right.

'Let her call us and apologize, if and when she realizes that she stood us up. When I tell her she missed a steak dinner, it will break her heart,' said Sy.

'This is her first semester here, and she's feeling her oats,' Carla said. 'I consider her my best friend, though she's been here only a few times since school started. She stayed with us for three weeks at the end of the summer. As kids, when we went to Grandmother Cassandra's in Telluride, we were inseparable. Can I get anyone coffee?' Carla asked. 'Or is it too late?' She stifled a yawn. 'So much talk. I have to get up early.'

Taking the hint, I stood and accepted my parka from Carla.

'Tomorrow always starts before you want it to,' said Sy.

Ben had a ten o'clock class on Wednesdays and politely conjectured that we would no doubt run across each other in the college library on campus. Carla had to open the swim shop at Trimble Hot Springs a few minutes before eight the next morning.

They no longer seemed concerned about Kate.

Though the company was fine and the steak at Lime Creek was thick and tender, the evening was an oddly unsatisfying one. I had not learned all that much from Sy — Kate seemed to know more than he did. A large piece of something was missing.

I hadn't been counting on seeing Kate that Tuesday, yet when she didn't arrive, I began missing her and found myself unable to concentrate on much else. It wasn't until I was back in my room and in bed that I understood why there was such an empty, hollow feeling to the night. I did fall asleep eventually, but was still wondering where Kate had gone; why hadn't she joined us? Was it because I was there? In a way, her absence, which made the evening seem so truncated, and empty, was as powerful as her presence would have been — only far more disquieting.

When I saw her later on in the week and asked where she'd been, she gave me that blank look of hers, which told me that it was none of my business.

'Is there someone else, Kate?'

'Don't be silly, of course not.'

Always the mystery girl.

Her absence still makes me feel heavy, now that I am alone.

•Seven•

As the weeks passed, I became accustomed to Kate's habit — her compulsion, really. She was entirely absorbed by her dead ancestors and, also, had a natural genealogical ability. Her stories and anecdotes were a model for her — a guide — and, to a large degree, governed her decisions and her behavior. For instance, when the inevitable problem arose between us about the difference in our ages — a twenty-seven-year spread — Kate brought in 'Uncle' Tom and his niece Helen DuVal, Kate's great great grandmother, as an example of a successful spring-autumn love affair.

It was mid-September, and she and I were with a few of her classmates on a field trip to Mesa Verde to visit the Anazasi ruins. Actually, I had tagged along and, though Kate and I were considered by her friends to be an item by this time, I still felt very much as if I were the old uncle to this young woman, especially when others her age were present. The day was hot, I remember, and after walking the ruin paths and climbing the ladders with our spry Park Service guide into Spruce Tree House and Cliff Palace and picnicking on the mesa by Sun Temple in the cedar and juniper trees, we were dry and dusty. Five kids were packed in my car. On the way home, Kate, Billy Hinkle, Sarah McCall, Betsy Waters and Steve, a young man who was dating Kate's roommate, voted on an impulsive stop for beer and a detour out of Mancos up the Dolores river to go swimming.

We drove along the river on a wide dirt road. Kate snuggled up next to me.

'When I was young,' she said, with no trace of irony, 'my cousin Carla and I visited Grandmother Cassandra in Telluride. She always wore a lace collar and had her hair piled high like a Gibson Girl. She served us lemonade and blueberry pie in her kitchen. The chairs were high-backed and hard. Once she took Carla and me way into the mountains to a hot springs near the Tomboy Mine, just the three of us all dressed up like ladies.'

'I wish I'd known you then,' I said.

Now Kate wore tight shorts and a tank top with, as usual, no bra.

'We sat on a blanket,' she said, 'in a meadow filled with flowers and looked just like a painting by Renoir, except we had high snow-capped mountains in the background. Cassandra let us wade up to our knees, but we had to keep our dresses on.'

I parked a short distance from a deserted pool.

Immediately, everyone, everyone that is except me, stripped and ran for the water. I spread a blanket a distance downstream and got undressed as far as my underwear. With age may come wisdom, but certainly not beauty. I was a white, fat satyr amongst that youth. Naked, Billy Hinkle was brown all over and his skin looked dusty. He was hung like a mule and paraded himself before my beautiful Kate, while I sat on the blanket in my cotton jockey shorts, penis shriveled to a gherkin.

The young people were not bashful with each other and acted as if their nudity were commonplace, which it was actually, considering they lived in a co-ed dorm at school and shared toilets, sinks, showers, and who knows what else.

Kate's hair was coal black — head, armpits and crotch. I had kissed every inch of that girl, and she said she wanted kisses from no one else, but still I did not find amusing her can-can dance with the other two girls.

I remained the prude in their eyes, I'm sure, because I swam alone in my underwear and did not splash and tickle. If I had done as they did, I would have seemed prurient somehow; by avoiding them I came off as a snob. There was no winning that one. I was an old fart, out of shape, bulge-bellied and balding.

What future could a sylph-like Kate have with me? I would be in a wheelchair at seventy and she would push me at forty-five. If we had children, my son would be saddled with a grandfather for a father. I would be dead before he finished grammar school. But, what bothered me the most was to see their world — their physical, sexual world — so separate from my own more modest and conservative one. The distance was never made more clear than it was as I watched those fine, naked, blithe students cavort from where I sat on the bank of the Dolores River — the river of sorrows.

Kate, young and brown, her breasts seemed to rise eagerly to drink in the light and the flashing water tossed at her by Billy Hinkle's large hands.

When she came over to me, I said, 'We should go soon. I'm wiped out. My feet hurt. I think I have arthritis.'

'You can't have that, Graden. Why, you're as healthy as a horse — better yet — an old goat. Come swimming with me.'

She smiled and hunkered close, pressing her breasts against my arm. Her closeness made me ache. The dark hair and her sex glistened.

'I have arthritis and I'll soon have dropsy and Alzheimer's and then a stroke that will paralyze half my face so I drool,' I said, lightly touching her breasts and her open legs. 'Please, let's go. I can't stand it. I want you so badly. Hurry, before I'm too old to know what I'm doing.'

'You fox, you. You sly animal. You just want to get me into bed.'

'Yes,' I said, helpless, overcome by her cheer and her energy and her blazing full youth. She was my light, my life.

'I want you. I want you forever as often as I can. Until I die. Please, Katie. Let's go home.'

She was young. She could not be expected to consider — not even for a flash — that I was just as young once. Oh yes, I remembered what it was. I had had my own time. But, I could not be like that any longer.

'Sure, we'll go. You old Mister Horny.'

And she stood above me now and placed one foot on either side of my hips and then pressed herself against my eager mouth — for a long moment — her tantalizing hands in my hair guided my face between her legs and held it there just long enough for me to taste and to give my love a quick and reflexive kiss before she skipped away to the others.

That evening, after drinks at The Barrel, we lay on her narrow bed in the trailer, tired — rather, I was tired — from making love. She was turned onto her side and pressed her body against mine. I took her breast in my hand and felt its warmth.

'What if Joe Aikin or his wife walked in on us. What would they think?'

'He knows we're here,' she said. 'He wouldn't think anything that he doesn't already.'

'And what's that?'

'That you're too old for me.'

'Or,' I said, 'that you're too young for me.'

'What do strangers think when they see us holding hands?'

'That I'm a child molester.'

'And, that I'm abused or retarded, maybe,' she said.

Then she laughed at my confusion and rolled on top of me.

She had a way — my Kate did — of moving her pelvis which immediately aroused me and she enjoyed talking when we began to make love. She talked and began working herself efficiently to get another release. There was a lot of need in her to release, after her naked cavorting and her free display of her charm that afternoon, all of which made her hungry and brimming with desire. And I tried mightily to satisfy that appetite and to a degree succeeded.

'Do you think you're too old for me?' she asked, moving on me.

Her hair was plastered on her forehead.

'You don't feel too old.' She sat erect now and placed her hands on my chest, moving as if riding Flame. 'Of course, you're not. My great great grandmother Helen DuVal was almost twenty years younger than her Uncle Tom. Well, seventeen years. Before him she went though a string of young suitors and had no trouble refusing them all, not after Uncle Tom.'

Kate moved slowly now, rising and letting herself down on me — posting, English-style. I held her waist and slowed her pace even more, to make this time last.

'My own suitors say they like my energy and my spirit. But I think it's my body they're after. What about you, Graden?'

'Spirit, energy, body,' I said, pulling her close to me now. 'All of you.'

'I haven't really gone for anyone but you,' she said, her breath ragged in my ear and mouth. 'Their hands were too soft. Helen DuVal didn't go for anyone but Uncle Tom. She said that the others were just boys who had no experience with quarter horses or heat.'

'I've had some,' I said. 'I can ride.'

'I know you can.'

She was coming now and rose up to gallop and threw back her head. And then I rolled her over onto her back where she scissored my waist and locked her ankles and began to move rapidly and eagerly for me.

•Eight•

One of the first stories Kate told me was that of Helen DuVal and Uncle Tom.

He was a cattle rancher from New Mexico who, after a number of visits with his niece Helen in St. Charles, became her lover. This was in 1888. She had both her children by him — Eleanor in 1890 and Maren in 1893. Eleanor DuVal, Kate's great grandmother, was the one who married the sadist Joseph Hodges and who died from syphilis. There was — according to Kate — no such cruelty between Helen and Tom. She did marry Jacob Stockett, but only to make the children legitimate, and she never had relations with him, as far as Kate knew from her reading of the family papers. When Helen died giving birth to the boy, Maren, Uncle Tom retreated to a cattle ranch near Santa Rosa, New Mexico, and later killed himself. Kate believed his heart was broken and that Helen and Tom should have run away together.

So that is why Kate believed there was not too great a gap in our ages. She knew it had worked — for the most part — a hundred years ago in her family, so she reasoned it would work for her and me.

Kate and I had been lovers for almost two months and by this time I knew the DuVal women almost as well as she did herself. There was a story for virtually every dilemma that faced us, and Kate took her family's solutions unto herself and followed them.

We were not too separate in age — not according to the DuVal myth — so that was that. However, regardless of her family myth, I was, in fact, too old for her. I realize that now.

When Kate was in diapers in 1971, I was just finishing business school. I was released from my first, childless marriage when Kate was taking her first steps. When she was in the second grade, I was an investment banker with my MBA and my first hundred thousand in the bank, and I was worth a half a million before she was sent away to prep school. Kate would not recognize that I had lived almost two and a half times longer than she had; it did not matter to her.

'Our hearts,' she said, 'listen to our hearts. They are singing together. Hear them? I feel secure with you — and also free. Don't screw us up by over-analyzing.' She ran her tongue behind my ear. 'Graden,' she whispered, 'you can't deny what you feel — what your body says — forget the other. Follow your heart.'

So, gladly, with reservations suppressed, I did so for as long as I could.

Yet, as I write now about that swim in the Dolores last September, with Kate's notebook of stories here open on the table in the trailer we shared for those brief months, I wonder if she had us in mind when she wrote of Susannah DuVal, her great great great grandmother, who had a lover during the Civil War. Kate cast her story in the first person, to allow Susannah to speak, but I hear Kate's own voice whenever I read the story and I call forth our romance and our excitement and, of course, see in that story an echo of what eventually happened between Kate and me. But, perhaps, I have begun as Kate did, to rely too much on Susannah DuVal's story, as well as the others, to explain Kate's and mine — letting her family lore take the weight of the explanation, when the cause may lie elsewhere, in a more raw and painful place.

Susannah DuVal's critical situation in 1865 was, of course, much different from Kate's when she wrote about her. Yet, Kate was my lover, and some of her feelings must have spilled over into her narrative, for whenever I read this section from the story, I am placed once again on the Dolores river. Her friends, the Yankees, are a distance away and Kate, like a muse, comes to me nude to soothe me, the old soldier who sits wounded with age on a blanket under a cottonwood tree in his underwear.

Kate, imagining the staunch yet tremulous sound of Susannah's voice, wrote of the young woman's first encounter with Volnoy Chaac, one of the men in her family whose part, for a time, I came to play.

This story about them is in Kate's black, three-ring binder.

She wrote:

In February, 1865, the Federals began a run on Tallahassee, approaching from the Gulf Coast to the south of St. Marks light. Word of danger reached us by the train up from St. Marks which signalled from the depot. We learned that two or three Colored Infantry Groups with white officers in command were marching up the river to Newport and planned in a few days time to move further north to take the capital.

The city, which had a year before been threatened from the north at Olustee, now prepared to defend itself from the south with a pick-up army. Captain Brokaw called the Home Guard from West Florida Seminary. Among those in the battle on March 6, 1865, was Volney Chase. This, the Battle of Natural Bridge, was my first experience in warfare at first hand.

During the encounter, my friend Susan Bradford's mother sent lunch baskets down from Pine Hill to be relayed further on to the battlefield for the soldiers. Other families were doing the same in hopes that none of theirs went hungry. In one of Mrs. Bradford's lunch baskets, I enclosed a note to Volney in which I told him that I prayed for his safe and victorious return.

Meanwhile, we girls waited at the train depot for news of the battle. In the distance, the big twelve-pound cannon which the Union army had captured the day before went off at regular intervals; the awful deep noise of its discharge carried from the point where the St. Marks River goes underground for an interval of a half mile all the way up the railroad to town. We waited all day. Around ten o'clock, the news came that the Union soldiers had suffered a defeat, and Susan and I left the train depot to hurry back to Pine Hill to share the good news with the Bradfords and, of course, to prepare for a victory concert.

The next evening, when Volney Chase, along with Captain Brokaw and General William Miller, called on Pine Hill, they were still quite jubilant over their success at Natural Bridge and invited all present to tour the battlefield.

'When we left,' Volney said to me, 'the Negro Yankees were piled upon one another all which-way, and the river was so covered with their floating bodies it looked like it was jammed up with logs. Our victory was a grand one, indeed it was. You all must see it for yourself.'

I hesitated to go until Volney suggested that I should pack a picnic for us and that we would make a full day's excursion, just the two of us. When I told Susan of my decision to go out with Volney Chase without a chaperon, she was not visibly concerned; it was our destination which made her bristle. She said to me, 'You have a heartless and gruesome nature, Susannah. How can you agree to such a thing?'

'I will go only in order to be with Volney,' I said. 'I simply will not look at anything that might upset me. Besides, I've not ever seen a field of battle.'

The following morning, at Volney's suggestion, I drove myself into town in one of the Bradford carriages and met him at the depot. Of course, I realized that it was out of the ordinary for a woman to meet a man unchaperoned, but it was quite ridiculous for him to hire a carriage and make the ten-mile drive to Pine Hill only to turn right around again and drive back to Tallahassee for us to catch the train to Natural Bridge. Why should he drive twenty miles to meet me when he could accomplish the same end by walking five hundred yards from his quarters to the depot? So we met in town. I handed the cloth-covered picnic basket to this solitary man with the freckles and bright red hair, the same Chase red hair which would be passed along to my daughter Helen.

Volney was respectable, if not rich, born of prominent people and, before we arrived at Natural Bridge, he appeared no less disoriented than any of the other soldiers suffering the after-shock of battle. He looked rumpled as if he had not slept well, yet seemed at ease and, certainly, grateful for my company. It was difficult to believe this gentle man with his easy smile had only days before been ruthless with the enemy. And I was quite proud to walk by his side along the platform. He was a fine man and noble, if made old by the war.

I must admit that I felt no conflict in my heart as I

sat beside him, even knowing that my lover, his brother Carl, lay ill. Perhaps, one would say that I should have taken Susan's advice and declined a private, unchaperoned picnic with Carl's brother, but Volney Chase's invitation was quite easy to accept and, besides, there was no one left on this earth to stop me from doing as I pleased.

We took the train to the spot where two days earlier the Home Guard had defended Tallahassee. There were no wounded. They had been taken away. All that remained was the battle-scarred ground and the grooved and carved trees that marked the conflict. We saw no floating Negroes. After we toured the battlefield, we picked a quiet spot to spread our blanket that was right on the Natural Bridge itself where the river flowed beneath us. I first put my ear upon the ground to try and hear the water flow and, recalling that time long since past, I believe I can hear it once again even now.

After we finished eating our lunch of fried chicken, peeled carrots, orange slices, and cornbread with molasses, he began to tell me of the battle there. Speaking in a ragged voice, he told me how he had recognized many of the soldiers as former slaves of his friends. He named a few — Ben, Big Tom, JT, Joe Junior, Snappy, Little Bill, Big Toe — all of whom he had watched die. In fact, he said that Snappy had called out to him just as he went down. Some of these Negroes I knew only by name, whereas others I had come to admire and respect and so was quite saddened to learn that they had fallen.

So distraught was I by Volney's remorse and overcome by my own frightening emotions, that I did not stop his hand when he rested it upon my ankle. He is a gentleman, I told myself, who will know when to stop. I would not have stopped him myself and have often asked myself, why not? Because the truth is that I was drawn to him as strongly as I was to his brother, though they were so different. He was not as swift as Carl and was less brutal, and I felt a tenderness in his heart which thrilled me. After we rose from the scattered remains of our picnic — and what a sight it was! — we did not speak of Carl. I was, or thought I was, no, I was much enraptured by this brother. Yet, Volney was so very strange. He had quite an unsettling effect on me. When we returned to the depot, I found that I was unable to manage the horses by myself and Volney brought me back to Pine Hill in proper fashion and then walked the ten miles back to his quarters.

Echoes. Granted, little more than echoes. Yet, I still see her rising out of the Dolores river, wet and glistening, to come to me. How her youth revived me. I could just as well have been blunted from battle fatigue as was Volney Chase. And how I loved her, loved her beyond reason.

Yet, just as our love did not last — though I believe we both wanted it to — neither did Susannah's and Volney's. In a way, what happened to them was ordained by Kate's sense of her own fate to happen to us.

Here is the end of Susannah's and Volney's love story, according to Kate:

We had been married two months. My child was due in three.

'I'm fed up,' Volney said to me one afternoon.

'Where will you go?'

'I will follow my other fellow, landless veterans,' he said. 'I will decamp for South America and seek a simple, new life in the remote mountains of Ecuador.'

'Volney, that's ridiculous!'

'Naturally, I promise to send for you and our child when I am established there,' he said, acting as if he had not heard my panic and fear.

'Of course, my darling,' I replied, hoping to change

his mind.

But, it was too late. His mind was set on leaving. I could not even think of going to Ecuador with him, and so I waited. Some time later Volney kept his promise and sent for me, pleading that I follow him. He described his arrival, his moving from Guayaquil where it rained for weeks on end, to Quito, the city built on top of a ridge, and finally his move to Otavalo where he bought a cabin by a lake. He invited me to come to him and he promised that I would find love and happiness with him forever after in this new life away from the ruins of the war.

I suppose that Volney knew it was unrealistic for him to expect a woman to raise her child in a six-by-six room filled only with his bed. Still, he described the rain and the chickens on his roof and the waterfall nearby. He made it all sound so much like the deep South before the War and, in a sense, he was living in slave quarters there in Ecuador. He named the familiar flowers for me — cinquefoil, chickweed, Indian paintbrush, purple and red vetches and flowers in the pea family. He named for me the stars: Orion was right overhead where he was, the same Orion which hangs low in our eastern sky at night over Tallahassee. He said that by morning he saw no constellations that he could name. He did not tell me of the slaughter-house smells in the streets, or of the urine and garbage and the manure or the pigs and raw sewage. He told me only of sweet cacao drying in the streets, of fried plantains and hot bread cooling near the stone ovens.

I adored his letter. It became wrinkled and stained and smeared. I must have read it twenty times, toying with the idea of going to him. I did realize I could not go there, not with a small child, no matter how deeply this Southern gentleman craved a simple native life with me, no matter how much he wanted a gentleman's woman to share his

life in the shelter of the snowcapped volcanoes in a
world of black skirts and black shawls and fireflies.
Without conscience he tempted me with food, knowing it was not plentiful at home. He wrote glowingly
of roast chicken and pork and rice, corn, potatoes,
beets, cucumbers, onions, celery, carrots. He evoked
the scenery — three enchanted lakes surrounded by
clouds and snow-capped mountains and eucalyptus
trees; he raved about the music that could be made
from playing armadillo shells, from flutes carved in
the shapes of fish and snakes; he wrote of goat skins
that sang; unashamed, he coaxed me with descrip-
tions of the churches and the festivals and the
Sunday market in Chordeleg which is also called
the city of gold.

If each of us had a critical time in our lives, then
April, 1865, was such a time for me. I was so torn.

It was ridiculous to even consider going. Impossible. And yet, finally, I said 'yes' to my husband. I
wrote to Volney and said, 'Yes, I will come to your
enchanted world, yes, I will bring with me the enchantment which once filled my womb and now sucks
at my breast. Yes, yes, I will gladly come to you. First,
I must know which port to book passage to and which
date you want me to arrive. Hurry and respond to
me, my dear one. Tell me quickly what it is that I
should do. Oh, yes! Certainly, I will come to you, my
love!'

It is a shame, but my letter never reached him.

However fanciful it may seem, I see my letter
fluttering like a white moth in the wind. It goes here
and there searching for a strange red-headed American, who is love-wounded and alone in that far-off
place. It settles, exhausted and forgotten, in some
far-away post office in Guayaquil and gathers dust.
And finally some efficient postal clerk returns it, long
after Volney has stopped expecting an answer from
me, much less an enthusiastic acceptance to his

invitation.

In any case, the letter never reached him; and I learned years later that after he waited for months to hear from me, he left Otavalo and went to work in the gold mines where his lungs weakened.

There my husband died in the gold fields of Ecuador sometime during the summer of 1869 and is buried somewhere in the mountains. He died without knowing that I had said 'yes.'

I have the letter here among my papers, worn from its long trip to Ecuador and back. When I received no word from my husband, I supposed that he had changed his mind. I could not stay on indefinitely with the Bradfords at Pine Hill, so I wrote to my sister Maureene who had discovered that in Denver a young, single, and passably good-looking woman on her own, caught up in the fever and abandon of a frontier town, could do best by doing one thing. Which my sister did.

At first I was reluctant to go there because I was afraid that moving to Colorado Territory might persuade me to enter the red velvet and polished brass and thick mattresses of my sister's profession.

I have since wondered who I was to Kate, which of those men she believed that I most resembled.

Was I her living 'Uncle' Tom who, as she says in her story of young Helen, 'never loved a woman more.' Or, was I rather her lost and misguided Volney Chase, longing dutifully, hoping his Susannah loved him enough to eventually say 'yes.'

I have fallen into her habit. My frame of reference has become as restricted as hers was in the end. I have begun to explain not only her actions, but also my own, according to her stories, accepting them, as Kate did, incorporating them into my life, our life.

*

In a large way, I was first her catalyst, a listener, the audience for her self-fulfilling role play. Later, I joined her troupe. How I wish I could have known the dangers waiting for her, for both of us.

Yet, at the time, at that particular time among many others, on the bank of the river of sorrows, while surrounded by the enemies of old age, I was made alive by her exuberant flesh and her bright love. I wanted nothing but her, no one but her. How eager I was to please her, to ease her worries. Of course, I would passionately assume any role which she wanted me to play — Uncle Tom, Volney Chase, Jacob Hodges. How ridiculous I must have seemed to others — the old, slack-bellied Civil War veteran in his underpants grasping for the breasts of a nymph.

We, however, did not seem ridiculous or pitiful, I am sure, at least not to ourselves. She had determined by then what role in her life I was to play, who I was, which of them I was like, and neither one of us ever looked upon the other with anything but joy and pleasure. It is I alone who looks upon us now, at some remove, with melancholy.

In the end, Kate would send me no letter saying 'yes.' If she did leave me anything at all by way of an explanation it is this notebook which holds her stories. And from them I hope one day not to hear her say 'yes' exactly, but to understand her 'why not.'

She left no explanation of why she left me — why she said 'no' to life, to this world. All that I have left of her are her stories and I must seek my answers — and what comfort I can find — in them.

Still, no matter how long or how hard I reflect, I have come to understand that I may never know much more than Volney Chase did as he, lonely and sick from miner's lung, hoped for the soothing reply from his wife Susannah, a promised and much-waited-for reply which never came.

•Nine•

Parents' Weekend. Kate was dreading it. Eva DuVal, her mother, had received the school's flyer and called to say that she would be there for the duration and that she wanted to attend a class with Ben Cooke on Friday, November 11th, and the opening reception that night, and the student coffee on Saturday morning, as well as the president's question-and-answer session, *and* the life-after-Fort Lewis panel.

'She's coming to man hunt,' said Kate, handing me the schedule. 'She'll cruise the campus like a shark.'

We sat at what had now become our usual table in The Barrel. Kate drank half of the Tequila Sunrise and motioned for more.

'You've got to help me with this,' she said. 'I hate to spend time alone with her. She asks too many questions.'

'Maybe she's interested.'

'Don't do that, Graden. You're not my father, remember.'

Kate had class on that Friday followed by a biology lab until seven, so I volunteered to take her mother to the opening reception.

Eva had booked a room at the Strater Hotel downtown and I arrived there well before six for a calming drink in the hotel saloon. Deafened by the ragtime piano music, I told myself that I was almost part of the family now, not just an old stranger. I was meeting my lover's mom and had every cause to be nervous.

I called Eva DuVal's room from the bar. She did not answer right away. When she finally picked up the phone on the seventh or eighth ring, I told her who I was and, also, as an ice-breaker, that I knew Sy and her niece Carla.

'Just how well do you know those people?' she asked.

'Not very. I've met them a few times. As a girl, you knew my grandmother Mattie Wells from Telluride. She had a candy store. I'm looking forward to meeting you.'

'I'm in three-twelve,' she said. 'Give me a minute to put something on.'

The staircase off the hotel lobby was polished, imported cherry with a cage-like elevator rising up its center. The cloth-covered walls were decorated with gilt, Victorian mirrors, and electrified gas lamps. The punishing, lively honkey-tonk from the saloon's piano filled the stairwell as I rose in the cage to the third floor.

Eva did not open the door immediately, but cracked it part-way until the safety chain inside went taut.

'Mr. Wells?' she asked. 'You are older than I thought you'd be.'

'I'm sorry. I don't mean to disappoint you.'

'Oh, you don't. Kate said you were a friend.'

The tip of her cigarette glowed; the hall lamps exposed a slice of her face and a strip of her dressing gown; when she closed the door to release the safety chain her fingernails flashed for a moment. She pulled open the door again and stepped back inviting me to enter the dark room, stuffy with smoke and perfume.

Kate's mother is three years older than I am. Five seven, like Kate, but she has short blonde hair, which surprised me. Her blue eyes are similar to her daughter's, but possibly not quite as warm or trusting. Not a cold woman, by any means, as Kate had led me to believe. Nor is Eva a hard woman. At least, I've never thought she was. Yet, a month from now, I would witness how hardened she can become by grief.

On the evening I met her, I found her nervous and, in her own way, maternal. At first, her frankness shocked me. Then I realized that, no doubt, the reason she talked so openly was because she lived alone and rarely got the chance to socialize.

'I believe Kate has found herself a man,' Eva said, 'and I know what he is like as a lover, how he makes her feel. Exactly. Kate's just like me.'

'You don't have to go into it,' I said, trying to hide my alarm. 'I know her fairly well.'

'Listen,' Eva said, rather sharply, 'I *do* have to go into it. She's my daughter.'

Then Eva offered me a drink and continued talking, as she left the room to dress in the bathroom.

'I had my first lover,' she said, 'when I was seventeen or eighteen; our lovemaking used to flash before me. I would have to stop what I was doing and hold onto something. It was so like a skyrocket, that brief time, so exciting and intense, and too brief. Yes. And when it ended, I wanted another one of those, and soon, one just as charged. Believe me I know, I know well, how my Katie is feeling. And I've taught her, no matter how much she's tempted, never to allow herself to be ruled by a man like her grandmother was, not by any man. She will not be ruled. Not Kate.'

She came up to me and turned her back, motioning that I was to close the zipper in her dress. The red piping on her dark green satin sheath matched her fingernails. Her skin was tanned and had a patina that resembled old furniture that had been waxed and polished by many hands. She had colored her lips to match her nails.

'How excited my Kate was to come here,' she said. 'Is she doing well? I set her free. Yes. I set her out on her own. I hope it was the right thing to do. I've seen to it that she has her own credit cards and money in her own account. And I've made it clear that she shouldn't visit out of duty, or call or write, never out of duty. She's probably all boisterous in her new freedom, but she was ready for it.'

Eva was pacing up and down, brushing her hair. Her voice echoed while she was in the bathroom.

She impressed me as a well-worn woman, yet wise and light-spirited. Somehow, she seemed to know even then that something was going to happen to her daughter. When she spoke of Kate, it was almost as if her daughter were already gone and that she had reconciled herself to that fact.

'At twelve, her eyes told men that she had experience, which could not possibly have been true. She misled some, especially older ones. She was not sophisticated enough then for the glances she gave men. She gave them, unwittingly, inviting looks. Sometimes I could not bear to watch the effect she had on men, even when she was ten years old. She provoked cruelty sometimes in even the kindest ones, just by looking, just by smiling. Men are, perhaps, her drug. I've seen that she has all the freedom she wants. I've made it possible for her to experience that which she did not know how to name. And she's always been a gypsy, anyway. Except nothing — no tribe, no man, no ritual — holds her back; not even I can hold her back, I couldn't even if I wanted to. I believe that girl knows no wrong and no evil.'

Eva went back into the bathroom. A plastic glass fell on the tile.

'Damn,' she yelled. 'I dropped my drink. Make me another, will you.'

After a brief search for her earrings, she went back into the bathroom again and closed the door. She had left her cigarette burning in its ashtray on the television set.

'She's my daughter,' Eva called over the noise of the toilet. 'Like me, Kate doesn't seduce men. She doesn't need to. She doesn't coax them or dance for them. Kate is sweet and strong and good. She's not helpless and submissive, like her grandmother was. No, Katie is not submissive that way. She's cheerful and playful. And it is unthinkable. It's absolutely unthinkable that any harm could come to her. I won't stand for it. Do you understand me, Mr. Wells?'

Eva looked stunning in her satin sheath and I told her so.

We took her red pickup to campus. I drove. At the welcoming reception in the student union, Eva was pressed with drinks offered by Kate's teachers and classmates, all of whom wanted to talk about her. I stayed at her side and was mistaken by a few as Kate's father.

'Our Kate has a delightful streak of play in her,' Ben said to Eva. 'Some call it a wild streak or an intractableness. But she's definitely not a trouble-maker. Yet she sticks out. Her classmates gravitate to her. She's a daring woman to them, with quick humor and an enchanting, self-assured way. Even her eagerness in class and her willingness to learn make her stand apart. She's an exception, Aunt Eva. She's her own person. She doesn't rebel, not exactly, yet she calls attention to herself without trying. And she's off center, or looks that way. She seems more free than most, willing to take a risk. When she isn't in a group, you ask, "Where's Kate, why isn't Katie here with us?"' Ben backed away from Eva and approached Sarah McCall, who was with her parents, dutifully making the rounds.

'God, what an absolute bore he is,' said Eva under her breath. She accepted a stuffed mushroom from one of the caterers.

Steve, who had gone to Mesa Verde with us, approached Eva. 'She's a party girl, really,' he said. 'But she has brains. It's nice to meet you, Missus DuVal.'

'It's not Missus,' she said, smiling at this muscular youth.

'She can be intellectually reckless,' said Dr. Bean of the English department when he stopped briefly to introduce himself. 'Her teacher tells me she's doing good work — family lore, I hear. Very nice.'

Miss Wilson, the Fort Lewis College librarian, followed Dr. Bean. She held out a gloved hand to Eva. 'Our Katie is so attentive and bright, so interested in her studies. So busy. She always seems to be on her way somewhere important. And she dresses so nicely. Now I see where she learned it.'

'I've lived with her for three months,' said her roommate Sarah McCall, 'and we are friends. But, you know, I can't say we're all that close. She has a private place inside her. That's the only way I can describe it. You can get only so close to Kate, that close but no closer. She's very private. I admire that.'

'She's really funny,' said the large Navajo Billy Hinkle. 'So, you're her mother?'

'Well, there's a lot of me in Kate, I suppose,' Eva said, smiling now. 'For all the good that does her.' She rested her hand on Billy Hinkle's arm 'Would you be a dear and get me a fresh vodka and ice.'

'Riding's really her true passion,' Eva said to me. 'Not school.'

'It seems to be,' I said. 'We've been out together once.'

As it turned out, after a walk through the dorm and

a few minutes in Ben Cooke's class and maybe a half an hour at the reception, Eva was content to stay close to the hotel for the rest of the weekend, receiving visitors. The friendships Kate had developed since August and the compliments Eva received about her daughter from various members of the faculty and the administration did not cheer Eva much.

I think she had the idea that the purpose of Parents' Weekend was for the school to get to know *her* better, rather than the other way around, and that she was disenchanted by the place and felt herself ignored.

So, she cornered me on more than one occasion and I found myself ensconced with my lover's mother, a woman of great beauty, one perhaps more appropriate for me than her daughter was.

After we left the reception Eva wanted to return to the hotel. Even as we rode up to her floor in the cage, she talked about her daughter. She assumed that I knew very little about Kate. But it wasn't until months later, after Kate had decided to stop seeing me for a time, that I understood why Eva told me what she did about Kate's spirit.

'You should know this about her,' she said. 'Last week I was looking after Katie's cat. And Kate came. Katie in spirit came right into the house. She does that. She went first to her room and then to the bathroom and watched me. Kate came to say goodbye to Ginger-bread. She was with me. I mean from way up here Kate knew her cat was dying and she came to help me.'

Eva had changed out of the satin dress and now wore a robe. She untied the sash and retied it tightly accentuating her waist and breasts.

'We both believe that a sentient being doesn't leave the world immediately after death,' she said. 'The soul stays here for at least a few hours. Gingerbread's soul stayed with me after she died.'

Eva went to the ice bucket and the bottle to make a drink, indicating that the bar was open.

'I was having coffee that morning. The cat howled and ran for the bathroom tub. When I went to find out why, I realized the house had Katie in it. I know how my house feels when Kate is there.'

Eva paced the room now. She moved closer and touched my arm briefly before going into the bathroom. The toilet flushed and she returned, removing a white blanket from the bed. She sat on the couch wrapped in the blanket with her feet pulled under her.

'The cat hadn't eaten. That morning — it was last Monday, no, Tuesday — she went into the bathroom and climbed into the tub, yelping like she was in pain.' Eva sat forward with her feet on the rug. 'We did what we could to help her.'

She moved off the couch, letting the blanket fall, and went to the telephone table to pour more to drink. I joined her.

'It was Katie, Katie's spirit, there with me, that made Gingerbread stop howling.

'I patted the cat while the poor thing huddled in the bathtub. I kneeled and waited, not knowing what I was supposed to see. Then I saw something leave her. Whatever it was left and went away. This didn't happen fast — more like this cloud rose out of her. Gingerbread's spirit left us. Her soul, her essence or her something, went away, and I was there to see it.'

Eva moved closer. She put her hand on my shoulder.

'I have never actually seen anyone die, Graden. I mean, I've never been there and seen what actually happens. I've seen plenty of dead things, but not like this, not as it was happening. That's as close as I've been.'

She drank again. She lit a cigarette and continued to talk, even as she exhaled smoke. She had her arms around herself and was rocking back and forth as if the memory made her cold.

'I wish she hadn't died. I know. That must sound

really obvious. But I so wish she hadn't gone away from me. I loved that cat. So did Kate.'

She finished her drink and held out her glass for me to pour her another. Eva was silent now. She blew smoke over her glass and looked at me and patted the couch cushion next to her, and I thought of a shark cruising, as Kate had warned. It was difficult to be certain if Eva was trying to seduce me or to test me, but I did not join her on the couch. There was something calculated in her talk about the dead cat and spirits.

Kate came to Eva's room after her biology lab and I was glad to leave for the Silver Spur.

•TEN•

In the morning, Kate called me early and asked me, please, to get there as soon as I could.

'Mother and I have had one of her serious discussions,' she said. 'This one was about you. And, oh, will you be an angel and go out to Aikins' and give Flame his carrots and hay. I can't possibly leave.'

I arrived later on and found Kate was alone in Eva's room. She seemed shaken. Eva had gone out for cigarettes, so we had a few minutes of privacy before we had to meet her mother in the hotel dining room for breakfast, as instructed. For the first time I saw how young Kate really was.

Our parents, of course, continue to treat us as the children we once were, and it takes us years to learn how not to regress. Kate had regressed. She was for now her mother's child.

When I took her in my arms, she kissed me and said
I smelled like horses. I said that I had given Flame
some carrots and let him nuzzle me. I realized that I did
smell of horses. She pressed herself close to me, and
gradually returned to the Kate I knew. She fumbled
with the buttons on my shirt to smell my skin, searching for the horse. Anxious that Eva would be waiting, I
moved away and began collecting glasses and newspa-
pers and picking up towels and emptying ashtrays. We
continued to touch one another as if to verify each
other's presence. We could not pull back. We were
separate, quiet with each other for a few minutes, then
without speaking, as two birds lift from a tree branch at
the same moment, we rushed toward one another.

Though the discussion Kate and Eva had had earlier
that morning was not mentioned at breakfast, knowing
what I did of Uncle Tom and Helen, I have a fairly good
notion of what transpired.

Kate wrote of the spring-autumn love between Tom
and her great great grandmother Helen DuVal, and
how Tom DuVal's sister, Maureene, expressed her weak
disapproval. I suspect that Kate's version of what was
and what was not said between Tom and his sister
resembles Eva's and Kate's discussion about us.

Here, then, is Kate's version of the scene in which
Maureene DuVal confronts her brother about his affair
with their niece, Helen. Kate wrote:

> 'There's nothing wrong with him,' Helen said. 'Noth-
> ing at all. Jacob [Stockett] is just fine. It's Tom. If I
> leave Saint Charles, then I won't see Uncle Tom
> again.'
> Soon afterwards, during one of Uncle Tom's long
> visits, Maureene was awakened by a dog's barking.

Then she heard someone tap on Uncle Tom's door which was across the hall from her own.

Maureene heard her niece ask, 'Are you awake? Are you sure?'

She heard her brother reply, 'Of course. Yes. It's all right. Of course, Helen, come in. What is it?'

Uncle Tom recorded in his memoir what transpired between his sister and him the next morning at breakfast:

'My sister waited til I had eaten before she spoke. Helen was not in the room.

' "What have you done to the poor girl?" she asked me. "You will ruin her."

' "Not so," I said, firmly. "Sister, I have never loved a woman more. How can that possibly ruin her?"

' "You will break her heart. She will be unfit for anyone after you. Do be gentle. I beg of you before God."

' "She will be even less fit, if we must stifle this. I have no course left to me, but to go on as we find ourselves or not to see you or Helen again, and the last I must say to you is something that I am not strong enough to bear." '

Whatever Maureene replied is lost to us, but Uncle Tom must have said to Helen that they both had Maureene's qualified blessing, if not her full approval, for there is no indication from Uncle Tom in his papers or in Helen's that they stopped, or even stifled their romance.

So, Maureene gave in to Helen's and Uncle Tom's love affair. She may have been right, for it seems that Maureene's only possible course of action was to caution her brother: 'Do be gentle.' It would seem that Uncle Tom and Helen got what they went after. There is something gentle here and loving. A trust existed, one not evident in any of the other DuVal women's love affairs. I hear the sound of footsteps in the hall, of quiet whisperings, then later came a formalized, domestic intimacy — not strife — between niece and uncle.

Such sentiment had not entered the lives of any of these women until now.

After that breakfast talk, Uncle Tom and Helen began openly to display their affection in front of Maureene and were less cautious about their interestingly sly noises at night. It seems they no longer needed to hide their love from her, and there is no record of Maureene trying to stop it, as if she could. Perhaps, Maureene knew that Helen would not find a stronger, a more loyal, a more loving man in all the world than her brother Uncle Tom. Then, perhaps, Maureene dismissed all of it, saying to herself that Helen was passing through a young girl's infatuation and her brother was making a passionate, last fling at youth; but Helen's love did not cool over the years, nor did Uncle Tom's ardor.

Uncle Tom's memoirs show that he would return to his ranch on the North Platte only when it was time for Jacob Stockett to make his visit; Stockett was still half trying to persuade Helen to move to the newly built house in Jacksonville, but Helen refused to leave.

Perhaps this arrangement was not as tense or as confusing or so like a soap opera, as I have made it out to be. Who can be certain?

Helen must have held Jacob Stockett in some kind of spell, or something.

He seems to have thrown away many of his own dreams — the lumber mill, the new house — so she could satisfy hers. I am certain that Stockett loved her — maybe in an extreme, dependent way — loved her a great deal more than she loved him — if she loved him at all. She was probably thankful or honored, but he must have suffered; oddly, I am tempted to pity him because of his devotion to her — that is, his inability (or unwillingness) to accept her refusal of his feelings and to leave her. I may be wrong, but I cannot help but believe that Helen wasn't selfish or cruel — she knew whom she most cared for and would not be swayed by devotion alone, or propriety. Yet I am disturbed by the pain she must have caused Jacob Stockett. Though somehow the pain seems to have been unavoidable.

Eva had coffee and an English muffin for breakfast. Kate and I shared an omelette.

Her mother, who now understood Kate's and my relationship, stepped right in, saying, 'What are your feelings toward my daughter?'

'I am in love with her,' I said, looking at Kate.

'Some Parents' Weekend,' said Eva, 'I come up here and find you two in each other's arms. I don't know what I think. What about you, Katie dear? Are you sure how you feel?'

'I am. Yes,' Kate said. She looked defiantly at Eva, not at me.

'And are you being careful?'

Her voice told both of us that she was concerned about disease (she thought, perhaps, that I had syphilis like Eleanor DuVal's husband Joseph Hodges) and pregnancy.

'Yes,' we both lied, dutifully in unison.

Myself, confronted by this woman, this mother, I felt an equal next to Kate. Two chastised children. But, really, I had no choice but to allow my lover's mother to call me onto the carpet as if I were Kate's age. Yet, I realized later, it wasn't so horrible or shameful — in fact, it made me feel almost spry and wild again.

As it happened, Eva condoned Kate's and my romance. She had been testing me the previous night with her touches and her looks and all. Though Eva didn't say aloud how long she guessed that Kate's affection for me would last. I bet she gave us no more than three months. From that time on I did my best to prove her wrong.

After Eva finished her coffee, she excused herself to go shopping. While we sat in the dining room, a couple dressed in matched leisure suits took a table near us.

'Which one of them started the twin routine, do you think?' I whispered to Katie.

'They both did, simultaneously.'

'Why do you say that?'

'This summer, after I got back from the family research trip mother sent me on, I stayed with Carla and Ben and Sy at the cabin and helped Elaine Frieze at the gate. They are so cute — Ben and Carla — like that couple there, like two peas, love birds. I bet they'll look alike when they're that old and that they'll wear identical leisure suits, too. I'm not going to be like that. It's way too co-dependent. What will happen when one of them dies? If Ben died first, what would Carla do? I'll bet she'd kill herself. He's all she has.'

'They're in love. In time, she'd probably get over it and find someone else.'

'Did you love your wife that much?' she asked me.

'I thought I did, once.'

'Are you over it? Are you glad you got divorced, so you could get on with your life? Don't you ever wonder where you'd be right now, if you were still married, or if you hadn't married her?'

'I wouldn't be here with you. I know that much.'

'And, if you never met me, you'd never know the difference, would you? See what I mean?'

'I don't know what you mean. I guess you don't want to love anyone that much, is that it?'

'I do. I want to love you. I do love you, Graden. But, I come first. I could never love the way Ben and Carla do. There's too much to lose. I can't give up that much of myself. Besides, what if I loved you with every single bit of my heart and then you died or you went away? That would be too awful. I'd never, ever get over it.'

'The way Sy feels about your grandmother?'

'Yes, exactly. Maybe Mother has the right idea. She loves, but not too much. She'll let someone come close, but not too close.'

'Do you really believe that? Is that how you want to live?'

'I do, yes. I think so.'

And, I asked her again up in Eva's room, as we made love in the enormous bathtub, if she thought someone could love too much. But I'm not certain that she understood what I meant. Perhaps you have to have reached a certain age to live the good lie, that is, to accept the basic impermanence in life while at the same time allowing yourself the faith that love will last forever.

There had been a few times when Kate and I had made love without protection. Kate said she could always tell when she was ovulating by a little stinging feeling or something in her side. Besides, we both agreed, who has ever heard of anyone getting pregnant in a bathtub full of hot water. With Eva condoning — if not entirely approving of — our love affair, I'm afraid that both of us were lax in the contraception department that morning, and after Parents' Weekend we stopped playing it safe altogether. We were, after all, very much in love and had Kate's mother's tacit approval.

For myself, I wanted a child by Kate. I remain uncertain what Kate herself wanted by me, but, if actions speak, then she wanted to have my child — at least she did for the time we lay together in the steaming tub in Eva DuVal's suite at the Strater Hotel during Parents' Weekend.

•Eleven•

After Parents' Weekend, for some reason Kate seemed to change.

She did not explain her sudden distancing from me, but what I thought had happened was that Eva had gotten to Kate and undermined us. After all, maybe Kate was more like her mother than I thought, preferring a string of men to a steady one. In any case, before Eva stepped into the picture, Kate and I had plans to spend all of our vacations together. I would have taken her anywhere — Cape Cod, New Zealand, Ecuador — but she took off for Santa Fe to be with her mother for Thanksgiving and left me to look after Flame and wait, and the entire time she was gone she never called.

I went to her trailer every day, stopping first at the Teepee's store in Hermosa for a few carrots before going to Aikin's place.

One evening Mrs. Aikin, who watched my persistent comings and going from her kitchen window, met me with Kate's freshly washed and folded sheets. On top was a towel from my motel, my toothbrush and Kate's overdue library books.

'Here,' she said. 'A sweet girl. I'm so sorry. Do you know that she rides Flame without a saddle. At first Joe and I worried about that, but she rides so well.' Mrs. Aikin followed me and continued talking as I carried Kate's books and my toothbrush and towel to the car. 'We said she could use the trailer as a getaway from school, but I have always discouraged her having overnight visitors. We thought you were an uncle until her mother told us differently.

'You see, Joe and I are gone a lot.'

She kept talking, and with my heart sinking and sinking I went inside the trailer and put Kate's sheets on the bed. Then I interrupted her to ask if I might feed some carrots to the horse or was Flame off-bounds too.

'We just can't have something unseemly going on,' she said.

After seeing to Flame's hay and carrots, I went for the Happy Hour at The Barrel and sat at the bar and drank beer and told Ned what was wrong. When a local builder, John Rowe, came in, Ned introduced us, saying that I wanted to build a love nest for my girlfriend.

'Her landlady doesn't like over-nighters,' said Ned.

Rowe and I had a few beers and quite soon he became the answer to my problem with Kate.

He'd fished at Electra Lake and knew my grandfather's property at the north end. One round of drinks led to another, and the next morning I went by Thorndike's Realty and took the land off the market.

By noon that day, Rowe and I were at the old cabin site taking measurements and developing a set of plans for a modest reconstruction which would retain most of the original cabin — the foundation and fireplace, half of the west and north walls, the two-holed privy. The interior would be insulated and finished in knotty pine, the exterior's wide rough boards and battens would be replaced and repaired. The chimney needed topping up and repointing. The windows were to be replaced and the well cleaned. The original tin roof would have to be completely replaced, insulated and sealed with plaster-board between the rafters to keep the original rough wood exposed. A one-room cabin — nothing fancy — twelve by sixteen. By early afternoon, Rowe and I had signed a 'time and materials' agreement.

Kate, I was certain, was going to love it. We would live in the place on weekends during school and move up there for the summer, away from the nosey Mrs. Aikin types.

'I'm not going to sell my land,' I told her after Thanks-giving. We were in The Barrel for Happy Hour. 'I took it off the market.'

'And you're going to develop, I suppose. You're going to ruin that beautiful place with huge lodges and cut roads right through the woods.'

'No lodges. No roads.'

'Are you going to move up there? You'll go crazy.'

'For the summer. Then, I might move to town in the late fall or go south — Tucson, maybe, or El Paso.'

She listened. She did sound excited for me, but I could almost tell what was on her mind. After all, I'd poured over the stories in Katie's notebook.

As I described my plans for the cabin, she as much as stuck a name tag on my shirt. 'Hello, I'm Jacob Stockett.'

And I played along and left the label where she'd put it.

You see, according to Kate, her great great grand-mother Helen DuVal went through a string of suitors, but had no trouble refusing them. They were more taken by her spirit and her appealing figure and her long red curls than she was by their too shiny boots.

Their hands were soft hands, and their lack of experience with quarter horses and with dust and heat and trail rides and rare afternoons in a meadow in the mountains made them less appealing. Whereas the life that Uncle Tom lived and described to her on his visits to St. Charles was what held her heart captive.

After one of Uncle Tom's visits, which lasted more than a month, during which time the two of them were inseparable, Helen decided to consider seriously the hand of one of her suitors. However, she told this young man (Jacob Stockett from Florida) that she would not leave St. Charles and go to Fernandina or even Jacksonville with him. If they were to marry, she said, they must make their life where they were — in St. Charles.

Unfortunately, Stockett was a lumberman by profession. In and around St. Charles there was not enough oak/hickory stands and too much cedar and bottom land hardwood; even the oak and short leaf pine stands were thin. If he were a coal miner, he said, that would be different, or if he raised hogs or made furniture or brooms or ploughs. He decided that Helen was afraid to leave the civilization of St. Charles for what was rumored to be a run-down, burned-out, rat-infested Jacksonville, still unreconstructed from its fires and destruction during the Union occupation.

So Stockett went there himself and built a house in the Fairfield section of Jacksonville near the ostrich farm. He set up a lumber mill on Trout Creek. But Helen would not budge from the house on Olive Street, not even after Stockett showed her specially commissioned photographs of the large house with its columns in front and portico and described the cut glass chandelier, lit by candles, in the entry hall.

She wanted to stay home, not because she was particularly dependent upon her aunt Maureene or because she was too timid to leave her own small home town for new territory and a new rough society. Nor was Helen afraid of Jacob Stockett. He is described by Uncle Tom as 'a tall man, a bit awkward at his joints, with a large mouth and hands and the softest eyes that I have ever seen on a man'. Helen enjoyed Jacob's companionship, even though he was clumsy at formal occasions and rough in his manners, enjoyed him more so than she did the younger men from more suitable families, who dressed well and who 'knew how to balance a saucer on a knee' and who rose with smooth elegance when a lady entered the parlor. Yet, no matter how kind he was, she would not leave St. Charles because of Uncle Tom.

To win Kate, I had done, on a smaller scale, just what Stockett did to try to win Helen: we both built a house to woo our women. Now, to help her make her decision, she brought forth Jacob Stockett. She stuck a name tag on my shirt; she saw what I wanted of her and made me into him, to more easily turn me down.

So, cautioned by her tale of Jacob Stockett, I didn't do what Stockett had done. I didn't ask Kate to move up to the cabin with me. I *know* she would have turned me down, just the way Helen DuVal turned down Stockett.

She fully expected me to ask her to live in the cabin with me. I know she expected it — expectation made her face grow hard and her eyes turn belligerently dark — and I was absolutely certain she'd say 'no,' that she liked it where she was in the trailer, and that she didn't want to be trapped in the woods at the far end of the lake.

'I hope you'll want to visit,' I said, as casually as I could manage. 'I'd like to have the place ready by early December.'

'That would be nice,' she said, with some disappointment. 'I'm glad you decided not to sell. I'm happy for you, Graden. I really am. I'm anxious to see it when it's finished.'

*

I had little to do with the actual reconstruction, except to approve change orders (which always raise the cost) and to pay the bills. I made an inspection once a week, more frequently at the beginning of the job, which was far less complicated than I thought it would be.

Each morning Rowe and his two helpers loaded the floating dock with the supplies and tools they needed for that day and towed it up the lake, returning at sunset with a load of scrap and trash. The dock held as much as a two-ton dump truck, with the plywood rails in place, and the added cost of doing the work over water was far less that it would have been to cut a road down from U.S. 550 across the Forest Service easement. Rowe had the cabin closed-in and roofed in two weeks and it took another three to finish off the inside — to set the sink and hook up the gas lights and haul in the gas refrigerator and stove. He brought in six tanks of propane, repaired the chimney and installed a new woodstove in the fireplace. He put new board siding on the outhouse and firmed its rock piers, anchored the dock with cables, cut and stacked five cords of pine and aspen, and raked the grounds. I signed off on the job in early December, well before the lake had even a skim of ice, and bought a used motorboat, hoping Kate and I would have a pre-Christmas weekend together, or at least a house warming there with the Cookes.

After the work was finished, I motored up alone, but spent just two nights there, because I was lonely in the woods without Kate.

'Spend at least some of your vacation with me,' I said.

We were in The Barrel. The only place we saw each other now was The Barrel.

'I want to powder ski,' she said. 'Billy Hinkle's dad has rented a condo in Alta. And then I want to go to the Mormon library in Salt Lake.'

'We can cross-country,' I said. 'The lake will be frozen

one of these days. And we'll get up there on a snowmobile.'

'I want to be with other people, with my friends. Don't push this, Graden. I mean it. It's my vacation.'

But I did push it.

'What about a long weekend after you get back?'

'Please. I don't want to.'

We finished our drinks in silence. We had run out of things to say to each other.

'I have to go,' she said. 'I should go study.'

'I'll call you.'

But she stopped returning my telephone calls. She stopped going to The Barrel for Happy Hour. When her room-mate answered the phone, she always said that Kate was off studying somewhere.

'Can't you take a hint?' said Sarah McCall. 'Most people can.'

'I just want to talk to her, that's all.'

After a few weeks of the cold shoulder, I stopped calling Kate. She left me hurt and lost.

After all, who wants to have anything to do with an old man who is love-sick over a nineteen-year-old. It's one thing if she wants to see him, but it's entirely different if she's freezing him out — for then he becomes not a rejected boyfriend but a pervert, a stalker, a degenerate. Which, I'm sure, is how Mrs. Aikin came to look upon me.

I would be better off, I knew, in the woods at my isolated cabin. There I could hole up without the temptation of a telephone or the possibility of a 'chance encounter'.

Yet it was impossible to give her up.

From Kate's stories, I know that Carla and Ben found each other only after a series of chance encounters, and Carla admits that after she'd known Ben for a few months those 'chance' crossings of each other's paths began to occur daily.

So I did not head for the woods, and went looking for

her in The Barrel every day.

What cinched it with Ben and Carla, at least according to Kate's story about them, was this:

One morning she was out riding Tess, and Ben was on the lake in his kayak. The boat was riding low in the water and he was paddling hard, rhythmically, smoothly, one side then the other, and looked terribly strong to her. Carla watched from the aspen grove on Vail Point. He paddled to the boathouse, almost a mile from Sy's dock, and began to cruise the western shore behind a group of ducks.

On mornings in late summer after the wind dies from the north, those high floating cumulus clouds can move in quickly from behind the Hermosa Cliffs and obscure the sun. The temperature drops ten or fifteen degrees suddenly, transforming a summer day.

That morning a thunderstorm caught both of them. Ben was still across the lake. Carla was in that shelter of aspen by the Cooke cabin. The wind rose white caps on the surface, and she saw that he was struggling against the wind and sudden cold, fighting his way back to the dock, nearly swamping the boat. Lightning strikes hit the cliffs and thunder rolled over them as the storm swept down from the north.

She waited in the trees until he had made it safely to the dock. Then she turned Tess and rode away in the storm. Ben may have felt her there, felt her before he saw the shape of a horse and rider wearing a dark poncho, moving down the road. He may not have known why she was there in the storm, at least not immediately.

A few minutes later he found tracks where a horse had turned on the pine needles and charged off down the road. He did not make the connection then, between the tracks and the black shape of Tess and Carla's poncho flapping in the storm. And Carla didn't tell him she was there, but waited until he figured it out for himself. And it took him a while to realize that the rider who watched to be certain that he got in safely from the storm was Carla DuVal on Tess and that she had ridden on the rain-swept road to be certain he was not swamped in that sudden, freak, blinding rain.

Then, after he found her tracks and after he knew why they were there and who had left them, his heart finally caught up to his mind — or rather, his heart allowed his mind to realize that he didn't want Carla to ride away from him like that, not ever, not ever again. And he told her so.

A month after his proposal, they were married on Vail Point. This was in 1985. Sy gave Ben and Carla the cabin for a wedding present, and they insisted that he live there with them. They have made it into a snug home. This winter, three years later, there has been no talk, as I have heard there was in past years, of moving into town before the first snow falls. Perhaps, one year, I'll have the strength of heart to winter in my cabin alone.

I had not seen Kate for almost two weeks when I went out to the Aikins' place. Forever vigilant, Mrs. Aikin stepped out onto her porch to stop me and I told her I would stay for just a minute.

Kate was not angry at my visit, but she did not invite me inside the trailer. The sun was set by this time and the wind off the river was cutting through my sweater.

'I think you've been avoiding me,' I said, talking through the screen. 'Why? What have I done?'

'I just can't see you for a while. I need some space. I want to see other people,' she said. 'My life is all confused right now.'

This string of excuses sounded half-hearted, as if she weren't doing what she really wanted, but what someone else was telling her to do. The trouble was, this time, I didn't know who her model was. Helen and Uncle Tom? Jacob Stockett and Maureene? Without knowing this, I didn't know how to respond to her.

'At least open the door,' I said, stomping my feet on the frozen ground. 'It's cold out here.'

'I can't. You know what will happen. You've got to stop coming here. Mrs. Aikin says no visitors or she'll throw me out.'

'Is it because I'm too old? Is that why?'

'Don't be silly. You're sweet. And I do like you. But I want us to be friends. We can't go on, Graden. I'm not ready to settle down yet. And you're too eager. You're more of a bonding-type person than I am.'

'Why are you doing this?'

'I'm not sure. To be myself.'

'Katie, please let me in.'

'I can't.'

'Why not?'

'Remember I told you about Cassandra's husband, John Pratt?'

'Of course, the guy with the turpentine camp who showed up at odd times and swept your grandmother off her feet. I won't do that this time, I promise.'

'Well, he had a wife who wanted to leave him. This was before he married my grandmother. And she stood in front of a train and John Pratt didn't see her again, not until she returned as a ghost. Graden, make it easy on yourself. Why don't you just pretend I've gone away.'

'Because I love you.'

'I know you do. I'm sorry. I don't want to hurt you. Just let me go for a while, so I can think things out. I'm not saying I won't come back.'

'Is something wrong? Is that it? Have I done something?'

'I just have to be by myself.'

'You're not pregnant, are you?'

'What makes you say that?'

'What else could be wrong?'

'I just want my own life. If you really love me, Graden, you'll let me have it.'

'But the cabin. I did it for you, Kate. Please, at least come and see it.'

She was silent now. Finished. She gently pushed the trailer's door closed and I heard it lock.

• PART II •

•TWELVE•

Perhaps my grandfather built his cabin for my grandmother, hoping that his wife Mattie would leave Telluride for the isolation and the two-holed privy over a stream. As I write this now, with Kate's presence, her smell, her things around me in her/our trailer, I can't believe that she had no intention of going there with me. What she wanted was some time alone to make up her mind to live with me.

When she pushed the trailer door closed and I heard it lock, I swore at her, at her entire God damn family — living and dead — and stepped away from the trailer, but at the same moment I realized that I had absolutely no desire — at least not then — to return to my cabin if I could not go there with her. The wind was stronger off the river now. I walked around the trailer and saw Kate moving inside behind the curtains above the sink. She would not look out the window, and as I stood there, scratching on the window screen, yelling at her to let me in, she turned out the lights.

Since I fell in love with Kate, I have not wanted anyone else. Since Kate, I have closed my eyes to all others. I have stopped looking. Even now, I still have blinders on my heart. I saw, still see, no one else but her. And no matter how hard I try, I most frequently cast her as Helen and myself as Uncle Tom.

No one could have foreseen the affection that developed between those two. Perhaps there was a natural attraction right along, or as Kate's great great grandmother matured, she might have brought something to Tom DuVal that he missed on the cattle range in what had been Red Cloud's territory, while he brought to her something that no man in St. Charles could bring.

Their devotion lasted all their lives. There is a photograph of them (which Kate had in her possession) — Uncle Tom stands next to Helen. He was forty-one at the time the photograph was made and Helen was twenty-four. I have a photograph of Kate and me and Flame taken in the barn. Flame's eyes look wild and red from the camera's flash.

Eleanor's brother Maren was born four months after Helen and Tom's photograph was taken in 1893. A few days later Helen DuVal died. After Helen's death, Tom went into the southwestern country where he looked after his land and cattle interests. For several years he lost himself in hard work, operating the Dubuque Cattle Company with headquarters at Las Vegas, New Mexico. Then in 1906, President Roosevelt appointed him Secretary for the New Mexico Territory.

This appointment placed Tom DuVal as an assistant to the five-man Court of Private Land Claims, which had been formed in 1891 to settle Spanish land grant disputes. As such, he had influence over permissions to the open range land in Colfax, Union, Mora and Harding counties in New Mexico, about thirty-five thousand square miles in all.

During his last years, he saw almost nothing of his sister Maureene because he stopped visiting St. Charles. I am certain that a part of Tom died with Helen.

Once in 1908, Maureene took Helen's children to visit him, and Eleanor and Maren would not forget this sad old man, their father, in his big hat on his big ranch in his big adobe house on the Carrizo river near Sofia, New Mexico, living all by himself. After he retired from the cattle business in 1910, Tom spent his time hunting birds. He was sitting on the porch swing at his ranch after a morning pheasant hunt, when he accidentally killed himself while he was cleaning his shotgun.

I want that story to be Kate's and mine — I will even accept the ending given a choice. But what it seemed to me that I had been given, though I hated to admit it, was Eva DuVal's story. For, when she closed the trailer door on me, I thought that I was nothing more to Kate than what the stock car racer, Wyatt Jones, or the half-assed preacher, Arnold Fosnot, was to Eva — one in a string, one who might have been the father of Eva's child. I believed my time with her was over, that her affection had run its course, that she was unattaching herself from me to go into solitude before finding someone else.

The last time I went to her trailer, on that cold night when she would not let me in and turned out the lights, I left Kate inside and went to Aikin's barn. Mrs. Aikin was waiting on her porch. She knew, I think, what I was doing in there, because this time she did not ask me to leave.

Flame recognized me and stepped forward in his

stall. He snorted and shook his head, not shying, when I slowly pulled out my handkerchief to blow my nose and clear my eyes.

I climbed into the stall with the horse and touched the animal's wet nose and rubbed his face and saw the sensitive frightened look in his eye, a look that changed slightly when I let him nuzzle against my chest to smell for the carrot in my shirt pocket. I spoke to the animal all the while, saying to him that it was not Kate's fault, and I understood, perhaps for the first time, how she could be so captivated by this horse, enough so to ride him without saddle or bridle over the frozen fields.

I fed the horse the carrot, saying to him it was not her fault, that it was no one's fault, no one's fault that she couldn't love me enough. I was unable to hold back the emotion that flooded through me during those last minutes with the horse. The beautiful, seemingly harmless, animal was now warm and nuzzling and slobbering on my sweater for more carrots. But there were no more.

I left the barn and went to my car. As I drove through the gate, I looked back and saw that Mrs. Aikin, who before had been decently watching me from her kitchen window, had left her house and was now crossing the yard walking toward Kate's trailer. I supposed that she went over there to console the girl.

After I left the Aikins' place that night, I went to The Barrel and stayed until it closed before making my way back to bed at the Silver Spur.

At one point, during a fitful sleep that night, in my dream I was a fly fisherman casting into a calm river pool which held a talking fish. She babbled to me. The fish was Kate. Then I realized that I was both the fly and the fisherman casting into the pool. As the trout lazily rose to inspect but not take the Royal Coachman, the dream broke.

There was a banging noise outside the room.

Immediately, my heart raced with panic, for the clattering and roar of machinery, together with the dream, made me certain that Kate was being dumped into one of the city's trash bins and would at any moment be compacted by the garbage truck.

I went to the window. The Royal Coachman and the talking rainbow trout in the dream were obliterated by the noise. I calmed down some. Yet a sense of urgency remained. I was still partially in the dream and wanted to command the trout to take the fly, now!

The truck finished with the Silver Spur bins and moved next door to the International House of Pancakes.

When it was quiet outside once again, the setting of the dream — like a painting — returned, but the fly floated undisturbed on the pool's surface film. The dream, and the sense of urgency that came with it, would float in the back of my mind for most of that day, an odd dream.

It was daybreak and out of the question to try and go back to sleep. The motel room was close and hot and my stomach was sour. I could barely eat toast at breakfast. Back in my room, I gathered a week's worth of dirty laundry and stuffed it into a pillow case and went in a sort of daze to the laundromat north of town, the one near Kate's trailer, a run-down place built on the bank of the Animas River. The manager paid no attention to me when I entered. Apparently he had just opened and was folding sheets with the help of a blonde woman in tight jeans and a snap-button shirt almost bursting with her breasts. She faced him over the stainless steel laundry table.

I loaded a washer and took a seat in front of the large picture window which frames the nest of mountain peaks in the distance with the Animas River in the

foreground. Not far from the river's edge is the Aikins'
familiar pine board barn with its rusty roof, the pile of
old hay and Kate's yellow house trailer.

Flame was not in his usual pasture close to the laundry.
And no heat waves rose from the stack on the roof of
Kate's trailer.

However, it did not occur to me then that Kate was
gone. If anything I thought she had gone for an early
ride and would return in time for school. She had finals
and papers due.

I dozed while my clothes went through the wash
cycle.

The blonde's laugh woke me and I moved my clothes
from the washer to the large, gas-fired dryer. The
laundryman made the blonde laugh again. They had
moved into the storage room. My shirts, socks, underwear, trousers began tumbling behind the dryer's glass
door. At one point, the laundryman left the blonde and
went down the row of roaring machines emptying the
coin boxes. He was dressed in a blue shirt and his long
dark hair was static-charged below his hat. He was
about thirty. I recognized him, nodded, and went outside to wait for the drying cycle to finish. I had nothing
at all to say to Price Jones. He was one of Kate's former
lovers, her cowboy. This cowboy-laundryman was the
one on her string before me. I leaned on the fence and
looked across the empty pasture at the yellow trailer.

Kate. She had listed the failed loves in her family so
often that I knew them all myself: Eva and her string of
men; Cassandra's stubborn refusal to accept Sy Cooke;
Eleanor, giving herself to the sadist Joseph Hodges;
Helen's death which broke Uncle Tom; Susannah's
pining for Volney Chase in Ecuador.

May and Carl Haffey lasted until May died, leaving

Carla's father alone. The only marriage left in the family was Ben's and Carla's, and Kate assumed that would break up, too, eventually.

What she thought of us, I'm not sure — I didn't want to be sure — but, in any event, what she thought would happen seemed to have happened. And I was left without her.

Maybe Kate was right after all. Maybe it's foolish to give such a large piece of one's heart to another. But, why live if we don't take the chance, even knowing that fate and finally death is against us. What else is there? How can I possibly regret loving her as I did, as I do. I wouldn't have it any other way, except to be with her still.

I went back inside to watch the dryer. When it stopped, I could hear, quite clearly, the laundryman and the blonde in the store room.

'I don't care what you think. It was nothing,' he said.

'She's too young for you. Besides, Price, what about me? Don't I count for anything? What am I? What?'

'You're important to me. God damn it. It's been over with her for months. I don't even see her anymore.'

'Really. You ended it just like that?'

'I was wrong. It was a mistake. It won't happen again. Okay? Oh, man. Can't you let it go, Carol? It happened. It's over. Forget it.'

'She has that trailer. It's too tempting. I bet you still sneak over there. I know you, Price.'

'I don't. It's done with. After me, she got the hots for some old guy from Boston. Now she's seeing a ski patrolman who blew into town. That's the way she is. We're finished.'

'You swear?'

'I swear to God, God damn it.'

'Prove it, then. Show me she doesn't mean anything to you, Price. Right now.'

'Here? I'm working for Christ's sake.'
'I mean it.'
'There's someone here.'
'Then you better make it quick. Hot stuff.'
'Carol.'
'Come on, cowboy.' She laughed then, with pleasure. Shirt snaps popped. 'That's it,' she said. 'Come on, come on.'

The laundryman and the blonde shut themselves in the storeroom and I pictured them making love on piles of swollen laundry bags. I had put my last quarter in the dryer and when it went off the t-shirts and cotton underwear were still damp, but I did not interrupt the reconciling couple for change and left the place with my clothes still damp.

· Thirteen ·

It was a gloomy morning. The sky was steel gray. Twelve days before Christmas. I had hoped to spend the holidays with Kate. But we had our final words about that.

We had had our final words.

I had left her at her trailer. In the dark. Maybe no one had done that to her before. Left *her*.

Dropped *her* like a stone.

I had been living at the Silver Spur Motel since August. I'd seen the county fair come and go, the Spanish Trails Fiesta, and the Iron Man bicycle race; I'd spent Thanksgiving alone at the International House of Pancakes because Kate went home. All this time, my feelings for her had intensified; I wanted to be with her more. She claimed that she wanted to be with me less. Maybe that will change, I thought, now that I have walked away, turned my back on her, pretending I no longer care.

I'd said goodbye to the horse, and walked. I would not be here waiting when she and Flame returned. Maybe, if I stopped running after her, then — just maybe. So, on my way back to the motel with the wet laundry on the back seat, I decided to take a drive. Only for a day or two. Until Kate came back and found me gone.

You see, at the time, I had no thought that she was in trouble. As far as I knew, she was off with Flame, hiding. Avoiding me for now.

So, I figured, when she came back and found me gone, then she'd realize how much she wanted me. Besides, the weather would be nice down south in New Mexico. It would be good to get away.

'So, you're leaving us, Mr. Wells,' the desk clerk said. 'We've enjoyed having you. I bet you're the longest staying guest the Silver Spur has ever had. You must feel this place is yours by now.'

'Not quite,' I said. 'I'll just be gone a night or two. Please hold my room for me.'

'Where are you going, may I ask? Do you want to leave an address?'

'I'm not sure,' I said.

I should have told him in case Kate came looking for me. I should have left word with Kate's room-mate or with the Cookes, with someone. I didn't realize until afterwards that she would think that I had abandoned her, which of course I didn't anymore than Tom abandoned Helen or Sy, Cassandra.

By nine that morning I was headed south, south into the 'Land of Enchantment', away from the sadness I felt about possibly losing her. For I believed that I might have lost her. Though I was filled with spite, resenting the Happy Hours I had spent waiting for her to show up at The Barrel, I still wanted her. Now she could stand a night or two waiting for me. But that was as far as it was supposed to go. I was angry with her.

Eventually, Kate would come out of her hole and find me gone and that would set her straight. She'd take for granted that I would be waiting for her, but I wouldn't be.

I continued driving through town to the south, where the countryside is bare and stark and extraordinarily beautiful, especially the long stretches of empty road, the anomalies in the barren landscape — a sudden volcanic peak, a stream. I made my small car strain mightily as it climbed out of the river valley and onto the high desert plateau south of town. Oil pressure twenty-five. Temperature hot, but not in the red zone. The steering pulled to the left. At Twin Crossings Trailer Park, I checked the tires. The left front was a few pounds low.

Between Durango and Aztec, following the Animas River, the cottonwoods were bare. Above the river, the hillsides held the ever gray-green haze of sagebrush and more brilliant dark green juniper. What I had come to appreciate most about this high desert country those past months was the changing light. Parched hillsides, golden slabs of barren rock, willow clusters at hillside springs. The air was dry. That morning the cold was intense, even in the winter sun, and I pictured Kate out riding Flame, while I was headed south.

The heat from the car's engine passed through the fire wall, through the soles of my shoes and kept my feet half warm. In the distance, to the northeast, yellow flames surrounded by auras of heat waves sprouted high from the gas wells outside of Bloomfield at the Blanco plant, the Kutz Canyon station, and from the barren flats of Angel Peak station. Wide, black-topped service roads cut off at right angles directly for the silver machinery of the natural gas and oil pumping stations. I was off the Southern Ute Reservation now and in the vast mineral-rich land east of the Navajo Reservation.

When one of the gas plants came into view, I slowed

down and drove in the break-down lane watching the gas burn-off shoot into the brilliant sky. The sound of combusting gases reached me some seconds after I saw the glaring yellow blossom and the envelope of blooming shimmering heat. A truck with a load of pipe passed, followed by a load of Navajos in a pickup, one that reminded me of Joe Aikin's truck. Without signalling, it turned onto an unmarked dusty road that headed for the seemingly empty interior of the reservation. In the truck bed were the grandparents and the grandchildren, the old ones bundled in rugs sitting in deck chairs facing backwards. I waved to a small boy in a bright red parka who was hanging over the tailgate watching the dust. The boy looked away to his dog, then to the old man. He did not return my greeting. Dust rose in a high motionless plume behind the truck. I saw no other living beings until I stopped at the trading post and cafe not far south of Bloomfield just before noon.

Parked in front was a familiar white Ford with a silver camper top. It had Colorado plates. My heart began to pound and continued to do so as I hurried into the cafe, not knowing what I was going to do. I felt a surge of panic come over me, the same feeling I had had that morning when the garbage truck woke me out of my dream. This anxiety had something to do with Kate, but I didn't know what it was and, certainly, didn't think that it was possible — not then — that she was in some way calling to me for help, that she needed me.

Inside, the customers were mostly Hispanics, along with a few Navajos and Pueblos, who looked up from their food to stare.

At first I didn't notice Joe and Mrs. Aikin seated at a table by the window. Joe called to me. They were just finishing an early dinner.

'What are you doing way down here?' he asked.

'Good day, Mister Wells,' said Mrs. Aikin.

'I'm just down for a ride,' I said, 'a change of scenery.'

'Is Kate with you?' asked Mrs. Aikin.

'No, ma'am. I haven't seen her since last night.'

'Well, good. We left her to care for Flame,' said Joe. 'She does a good job of that. We're off to Albuquerque for the rest of the week.'

'I was sorry to learn about you two,' said Mrs. Aikin. 'She was some upset last night after you left.'

'I believe the girl cares for you,' said Joe. 'The Missus didn't understand that before.'

'I settled her down the best I could after you left. You'll be going back, I hope.' she said. 'I didn't realize. . . .'

'I needed some air,' I said, as calmly as I could manage. 'Is she all right?'

'She was better early this morning when we left. I think you surprised her walking away like that. I might have judged you a little too harshly. We wouldn't want to be the cause of something,' said Mrs. Aikin.

'I'm sure you're not,' I said, excusing myself to take a table away from them.

I ordered a tamale plate and coffee. Soon another white Ford pulled up and parked along side the Aikins'. Two young Navajos climbed out. They were pulling a horse trailer that had a roan inside. I was eating my tamale with green chili sauce when the Aikins rose from their table and paid. Joe nodded to me on the way out.

'Don't stay gone too long,' he said. 'Come and see us.'

Perhaps it was at that moment that I realized I was fooling myself to think that I could blithely drive through this open, barren land and stop at a roadside cafe and not be reminded of Kate. For me, she was everywhere. I could think of no one else.

I signalled to the waitress for the check. She looked at my half-eaten tamale and asked if everything was all right.

'Nothing's wrong,' I said, 'It's just that I've lost track of time and hoped to get to Grants and back north before dark. I'd like my check and a large coffee to go.'

She was a pretty girl, as young as Kate, dark skinned with flashing eyes — like Kate's eyes, I realized. She was flirting with an old rancher between customers.

She set down my coffee and check and went back to the counter to continue flashing her eyes. The old man wore a white shirt and didn't take off his hat to eat. He touched her hand. She pulled on his hat brim and laughed. And that was when I knew instinctively, without reservation, Kate did want me. We couldn't get along without each other. Not to be with her was unthinkable. I left the money on the table and went to the outside telephone. I knew nothing specific, only that Kate wanted me. I don't know how I knew this, but I did.

The trout in my dream had risen to the fly.

First, I called Kate's dorm at the college and the Cooke cabin, but got no response. I stood at the phone for a moment in the dust outside the cafe, unable to think where I should call next. Then I drove north, back-tracking. At Aztec, an hour later, I stopped for gas. The tire was low again and the radiator needed fluid. It was almost one o'clock by this time — an hour's drive remained. Now I was hungry and took a cold tuna sandwich and a pickled egg from the station's cooler.

From Santa Fe information I got Eva DuVal's number. Probably she was the only person who could understand this premonition of mine, with her talk of spirits and such. Besides Kate might have called home, though I doubted it. All I knew was that the fly, the Royal Coachman in my dream, was me and the fish was Kate, and that she had taken the fly. Because of this, I felt sure that for some reason she was in some sort of trouble.

I dialed Eva's number and she picked up before the phone had a chance to ring.

'Eva,' I said. 'Hello? Is that you?'

'Graden, I was napping and something, Kate, woke me up. God, I have this awful neck ache. Something's happened to her.'

'That's why I'm calling. I think so, too. But I don't know where she is. Have you seen her?'

'No. She was here,' said Eva. 'She visited me and woke me up just before you called.' A low moan escaped her. 'My neck hurts. Graden, can't you do something? You must know where she is.'

And Eva began to cry. She said nothing more to me. I heard the telephone receiver clatter onto the floor. Eva was saying Kate's name over and over.

'Kate. Oh, Kate! No! No! No! Not you!'

I yelled, but Eva did not pick up the receiver.

After a few minutes, I broke the connection and quickly called Trimble Hot Springs and got Carla in the swim shop.

'It's Kate. She's in some kind of trouble,' I said. 'I've just talked with Eva. She said something about Kate being there, but she couldn't be. I saw her last night. Eva thinks that Kate is hurt.'

'Where are you?'

'I'm in Aztec.'

'What are you doing down there?'

'This morning I started driving and, well, I'm on my way back. She's in trouble, Carla.'

'What's wrong?'

'I'm not sure. Nothing serious, I hope. I think she needs me, but I can't find her.'

'How do you know she's in trouble?'

'I don't, not for certain. I have this feeling that something might be wrong. She wasn't at her trailer this morning and the Aikins' horse was gone.'

'I thought you weren't seeing each other any more.'

'I did too. But I ran into Joe Aikin and his wife, and she said Kate was upset. So I called Eva. She's. . . . '

'Graden, I know this has been hard for you. But Kate is Kate. She's still young.'

'It's not that. Will you have Ben check at school?'

'She has his class this afternoon. I'll tell him. But I

think you're imagining this, Graden.'

'Just ask Ben to be sure she's at school. I'll go up there when I get back.'

It made no logical sense, really. At least, I know Carla thought it didn't. Even now I'm not sure how I knew what I did. Carla was curt with me, disapproving, as she had been the first time we'd met.

'Try and settle down, Graden,' she said. 'I'm sure she'll be in class. I've got people waiting.'

I called Eva again, but her line was busy.

Suddenly, all this seemed my fault. According to Mrs. Aikin, Kate was distraught. Because of me she might have harmed herself. But, what had I done, after all? Except to love her. She made me mad, so I left town to clear my head. There was no question that I needed her much more than she needed me, yet I was prepared to let her go, to do what she pleased, to do anything, just as long as she fitted me into her life. I did not want to live without her and would compromise on anything, just so she didn't shut me out entirely. So what? Maybe I had left angry, but now I was back-tracking, returning to her, prepared to beg, praying she wasn't hurt.

•FOURTEEN•

I arrived in town an hour later and went immediately up the hill to the college. Kate was not in her
dorm room. Ben's class started in half an hour, so I
looked for Kate in the library. I was about to ask the
reference assistant if she'd seen Kate, when Miss Wilson,
the librarian, hung up the phone and said to both of us,
'One of our students seems to be missing.'

'Who?' I asked, knowing the answer.

'Kate DuVal. The girl we set aside the books for —
Webb's *History of Florida* and *Rio Frio Escapades* by
Alan Brand.'

'The one with long black hair? That handsome girl?'
asked the assistant.

'Yes,' said Miss Wilson, 'the president's office just
called to warn us to expect an assembly in a few
minutes.'

'Oh, Kate,' I said. 'I knew it.'

The blood rushed to my stomach.

'She's Professor Cooke's student, isn't she?' said Miss Wilson.

'Ben's wife, Carla, is her cousin,' I said.

'She's been working like a house-a-fire on her family history,' Miss Wilson said to me. 'We've sent away for book after book. Her final paper is due this week. It's very unlike her not to come in, especially now that her books have arrived. These new ones are on loan from Tallahassee and San Antonio. I hope something hasn't happened to her.'

'I sent her the book arrival slip on Saturday afternoon,' said the assistant. 'I thought she'd want to work Sunday, what with so little time left.'

'Such an interesting young woman,' said Miss Wilson. 'I've taken a rather special interest in her and her project, I must admit. She's studying the women in her family. Such a life they had. Quite an ambitious project, indeed, for a freshman.'

'Are you a relative?' the assistant asked me.

At that point, we were interrupted by the call to assembly, and I rushed from the library in search of a bathroom. When I returned, the library was locked. The halls were quiet.

And, outside, the campus looked abandoned. The entire school was at assembly. As I was walking to the lot for my car, Ben Cooke pulled in and I signalled to him. He veered across the blacktop heading toward me. We walked across the grass to the humanities building together. Carla had told him what I'd said about Kate.

'I'm worried,' I said. 'So is Eva. I saw her last night at Joe Aikin's trailer. We had a little fight, so I left. I thought she wanted to break up. But I guess she didn't. At least, that's what Missus Aikin told me. She was gone this morning.'

Ben didn't believe Kate was missing.

'It hasn't been twenty-four hours,' he said. 'She's probably off someplace.'

'I know,' I said, 'but, she didn't check out of her dorm on Saturday night and hasn't been seen here since. So, according to the administration, she's been gone since then. That qualifies her as missing. God, what a mess. Something's wrong, Ben. I can feel it.'

When we passed the gym and the doors swung open, what looked like the entire student body spilled out. In the crowd was Billy Hinkle, who had invited Kate to join him at his condo near Alta over Christmas to ski the dry powder.

'Hey, Doctor Cooke,' said Billy, 'what do you think about Katie? We just heard at assembly that she's maybe missing. Not for sure. It's just that nobody's seen her. You don't get lost at this school. What do you think happened to her? President Laws asked us to continue our normal activities, but to keep an eye out for her, you know, like in the library stacks and the student lounge.'

'Kate? Our Kate? Missing?' Ben asked him. 'That's ridiculous. Are you certain?'

'Sir?' Billy's eyes flashed momentarily with a challenging anger. 'The authorities have been notified to begin a search.'

'Sorry,' said Ben, backing off. 'You're not kidding me, are you?' Then he said to him, gently, 'She's my wife's cousin.'

'No, sir. I'm quite serious. None of us has seen her since Saturday night.'

'I have,' I said. 'Last night.'

Billy Hinkle tagged along with Ben and me.

While we stood before the humanities building, Joe Bean, the English department chairman, approached. 'You heard about it then?' Bean asked. 'I think it's nonsense and premature and will cause panic and distraction among the students, but it's done now. They're calling her "misplaced," not "missing," as if she were a lost object.'

We left Ben's department chairman standing in a swirl of curious students and went to President Law's office. The president's secretary, who had spoken with Eva DuVal earlier, said that the girl's mother had no idea if Kate was planning a trip or not.

'Her room-mate mentioned something about a man,' said Miss Hibbard, who was Irish and had a lilt to her voice, so everything she said, no matter how unhappy or distressing, sounded full of cheer. 'She was last seen with a man, a ski bum I heard, in town, she was, on Saturday evening. Maybe he was a relative. Her mother called us before we called her. She's certain Kate's in harm's way and wants to come up here, she does. But President Laws thinks not, it's not wise. Not wise at all. He wants her to stay where she is close to the telephone, in case our Katie calls. And security is contacting all the hospitals and fire stations and police stations within a hundred miles, a hundred mile radius. That's as far south as Shiprock and east beyond Pagosa Springs and west beyond Mesa Verde and, my goodness, as far north as Ouray. Security is going to run itself a huge long-distance bill on this one, you can be sure of that.

'It's exam time, you know, Professor Cooke. And final papers are due. The students sleep anywhere and everywhere at the end of the term, they do. The girl's not lost, no, she isn't lost. Not Kate. She's asleep somewhere right under our noses. She's somewhere quite close. She's close at hand, and we'll all look like fools if we let this grow into a general panic and let it out that we have a missing girl on our hands, no, sir, we can't have her going missing, after all, before we know it, her picture and the school's good name will be smeared all over a million milk cartons. And President Laws is concerned about admissions. He is, understandably. The poor little bunny's dead tired from studying and has dropped off somewhere. We'll find her.'

Ben's English class was waiting for him. I stayed outside the classroom in the hall while he returned papers. Then we went to his office. By late afternoon the possibilities of locating Kate on campus seemed exhausted. She had missed all her classes. No one had seen her, not even her room-mate. She had not been to the cafeteria. It had been forty-eight hours since she was last sighted on campus. I wondered if Kate had any other family that she might have gone to visit.

'Her only family is Carla and Eva,' said Ben. 'No father. No other cousins.'

At the end of the day a group of students came to Ben's office to lodge a formal protest. They demanded to know what the administration was doing for Kate. Most were certain she was in some kind of trouble and faulted the school for hesitating to act, for refusing to admit their friend was missing. Kate's room-mate, Sarah McCall, was by this time convinced that she had been kidnapped or killed and wanted to know why Ben, personally, wasn't doing anything about it.

Ben tried to pacify the students, but could only offer the vague explanation that this was private, an emergency, a family matter.

'I will not discuss Kate with them,' said Ben. 'The excitement and expectancy of these kids, their damn morbid curiosity and stupid theories of what happened alarm me, yes, and have me almost convinced, without evidence, that something is wrong.'

Ben and I left campus at four fifteen. There was no mention of Kate DuVal on the local news, nothing in the paper. I was following his gold van.

Of course, my persistent thought was that Kate wasn't really missing. She'd simply gone off somewhere to be alone, gone off to be rid of me. If she was hurt, as Eva believed, she was hurt emotionally. I said nothing of this to anyone. After all, I still believed that Kate had refused me, and I didn't want to admit that. So, however ingenuous it was of me, I went along with the search, knowing full well she was not lost, but had run. Kate could not simply disappear.

Initially, she had run, I believed, as her great grandmother Eleanor had run from that sadist Joseph Hodges, who gave her syphilis at his lumbermill in Oak Hill, Florida. But I don't think it was Eleanor, not this time. It seemed to me more likely that she was imitating John Pratt's first wife, Sarah, the one who stood in front of a train in order to leave her husband.

The railroad tracks passed near Pratt's camp in Georgia; and, so the story goes, Sarah Pratt left the house or shack or shed where Pratt kept her and followed the spur which led to the main line to Atlanta. There she waited for the train to come through. Which it did, eventually, not even slowing down, not even blowing its horn. One minute Sarah Pratt was standing on the tracks holding her baby, looking at John Pratt with hate-filled eyes. She wore her white cotton nightgown buttoned up at the neck, her hair was unpinned and almost floating off her shoulders from the wind that the train pushed at her as it got up close. The baby was in a gown Sarah had sewn from a bean sack.

And the next moment the train went through; a long train with maybe a hundred or a hundred and fifty cars to it. When it finished going through, Sarah Pratt wasn't standing there anymore. She had been picked up by that train and carried away, she and her baby, carried away to a better, or at least to a different world, one without Pratt.

I believed that Kate was imitating Sarah, the one who would return to Pratt later as a ghost with her ghost child. Kate was Sarah, and she had cast me as John Pratt, Kate's grandmother Cassandra's persistent lover, the one who knocked on screen doors and disrupted lives. Even though she cared for me, as Joe Aikin had said, for now, I was one to be avoided.

No. Kate was not missing. That would be unthinkable. She was hurt and was hiding from me, the way Sarah Pratt hid from her husband until she returned to him as a ghost with a ghost child.

•Fifteen•

I followed the Cookes' van off campus and out
of town. Most of the string of motels on the North
Main strip flashed 'Vacancy.' Kate had credit cards
and could easily be holed up in any one of those
places. We went north on U.S. 550 and, without re-
ducing speed, cut east on the lake road. My car
rumbled close behind the van, passing through a
series of potholes in front of the tin-roofed log house
and barn where Carla's father kept his horses. Sway-
ing and rattling, the wheels slammed into the fender
wells. The vehicle sent out billows of dust into the face
of a black dog, Kate's free-roaming bitch Bessie, which
she had brought with her to school and turned loose
at the lake; she ran after us barking into the darkness, dust and exhaust. The van continued for a mile
or so through a small valley before it circled back

south and began the short climb to the lake's gate-house. There, the thick dust cloud caught up with us and passed over our vehicles to continue moving forward, over the rise to Electra Lake, which was by now a sheet of thick black ice.

When our own dust had cleared, Elaine came out of the gatehouse pulling on her jacket. She unhooked the barricade across the road and watched it rise into the pine boughs.

I stopped for a moment to talk to Elaine Frieze. She told me that before school had started that fall and now on some weekends, Kate helped her look after the gate.

'Usually she wore tight shorts and a red bandanna halter,' Elaine said. 'That stopped the fishermen cold. And when they kicked up too much dust, she stood on the road with her hands on her hips glaring in disgust as their dust clouds blew over her. Finally, that girl set up a sprinkler and watered this section of road and she kept the water on it until the fishing traffic died down in the late afternoon.'

I couldn't bring myself to tell her Kate was missing.

As I approached the frozen lake, I began to drive more slowly, following a set of wheel ruts along the shore line. At Vail Point, Ben stopped the van at their side road and stepped out to unlock the chain, letting it drop. Sy had seen us coming and stood at the cabin's open door. In the porch light, the two men's similarities showed — they have the same eagle's beak for noses and the same wild eyebrows. The old man has blue eyes; the younger one's now were dark green.

'Hey, get my hat,' Sy called. 'I must have left it in the van.'

I retrieved the worn Stetson from the van's floor and hurried after Ben in the cold.

As we pushed into the cabin, Carla nodded to Ben and then to me; she searched our faces for news. Her smile quickly left her.

'Right after you called,' she said to me, 'I got this

feeling that something wasn't right.' Her gentle eyes searched mine. When I evaded her look, she moved closer to Ben.

'Do you think it's serious?' she asked him.

'Yes,' said Ben. 'I'm afraid this time it is.'

Her eyelids fluttered, as if she was experiencing a sharp pain. Her eyes spoke her worry first — her honest, sad, huckleberry eyes. She got up from the couch.

'I've been trying to reach Eva all day. First the phone is busy and then there's no answer.'

While Carla was on the telephone, Sy took me aside and said: 'I've known waiting like this one time before in my life, when I went in search of Carla's grandmother Cassandra because I loved her. It's pure hell. I was twenty. An understanding old woman named Maureene DuVal helped me get through it. She was Cassandra's great great aunt. I have always been thankful to Maureene for her help. It looks to me like you could use some help now.'

'Hello, Eva? Is that you?' Carla asked. 'You sound funny.'

I listened to Carla as she talked with Eva in Santa Fe. She spoke softly into the mouthpiece. 'We're doing all we can on this end, Aunt Eva. I think the school is right. You should stay there in case she comes home,' Carla said. 'How can you be so sure? Eva, she's all right. What on earth could have happened to her? Try not to worry.'

The telephone call with Eva was going to last a while, so I put on my coat, preparing to leave. Sy stood and put on his.

'Let me talk to you for a minute,' he said. 'Outside.'

The wind was bitter. So we took shelter in my car and turned on the heater.

'When I said that I've had my turn at waiting,' Sy

began. 'I was talking about Kate's grandmother Cassandra. I waited all my life for her.'

I did not reply, knowing something of the story from Kate, and after all, Sy had written a song about this, 'Slow Fires.'

He said, 'When I was in Denver in 1929, at the age of twenty, I had already made up my mind that Kate's grandmother was going to be my wife. I'd known her since I was small. We were playmates in Denver during the years that her mother Eleanor worked for my mother as her housekeeper.'

I turned the heater fan down a notch to hear him better. By this time, the windows had begun to turn white with frost.

'It was one of those things I knew,' he said, 'or thought I knew, for certain. Even after Cassandra went away, when I began trail riding in New Mexico, I kept her as the vision I had of a wife. You might call her my dream wife. I had her frozen in my mind. She was there just waiting for me to decide when the right moment was.

'In fact, I had no idea what was in her heart or mind, no idea at all. When Cassandra's brother Elliot moved west to work with his father Bill Ramsey, this woke me up and set me in motion towards her. Elliot's arrival determined me to waste no more time and I went after her. Perhaps I noticed that her younger brother was full grown and that gave me a panic, you know, that time was wasting. But, with Elliot's arrival there sure did come the panic. The feeling I had before of a cozy certainty about Cassandra's and my future was suddenly thrown into turmoil. Still, I was determined that it was time for me to marry her, and I wrote her a note to that point, but I didn't take into account that Cassandra was grown up now, more so than her younger brother, and capable of making her own life without even thinking about — or without even remembering — me.

'Still, I left Denver for St. Charles by train to propose. My trail riding job with the New Mexico Cattle Association was being held for me. The heavy leather wallet in my coat contained five hundred dollars and a round trip ticket, plus a one-way for Cassandra. I left in anxious, but high spirits, believing that my timing was perfect; I did not run to her, but went with all the confidence of a man who knows what he wants and is about to get it. I was off East to bring back my bride, who was waiting up nights, anxious for my arrival. Or, so I believed.

'On that train ride East, I stayed awake, going over what I was going to say to her, carefully framing my proposal in my mind. I saw her as a tall and slender woman with black hair and dark eyes, who was called independent and who was said to like men, but who could made do just fine without them. And I arrived carrying a Gladstone bag that had been my father's and I wore a new wide brimmed Stetson which was creased and crumpled by the time the train pulled into Saint Charles. If I was sure of myself when I left Denver, that certainty had fled by the time I faced the DuVals' big yellow house with its white picket fence on Olive Street.

'I was met at the door by a house servant,' he said. 'She didn't know who I was, nor was I expected. She left me on the veranda like a damn carpet bagger holding a bouquet of cut flowers while she went in and got the nurse.

' "Cassandra is not here," said the nurse. "She's gone. There's no one here now, but old Missus DuVal."

' "Where did she go?" I looked at the flowers, I remember, and then impulsively handed them to the nurse.

' "I'm not sure. She'll know, I suspect. Missus DuVal will know."

' "Is it possible to see her?"

' "She's not well. She's not well at all. She's tired and worried and alone in this great big house. I'll ask if she'll see you."

'The nurse disappeared into the house. I set down my bag and waited. The garden below me, off the veranda, was just coming into bloom and the sour smell from the wide, slow-moving Missouri river was strange and new. All that water.

'After a few minutes, the nurse returned and showed me into Maureene DuVal's bedroom. My flowers had been put into a vase and were on her dressing table next to the photograph of Helen and Uncle Tom that was taken in eighteen ninety-three, when she was pregnant with the boy, Maren. Maureene lay there alert and sharp-eyed. She looked held down by the weight of her quilted comforter. I had never seen anyone so fragile looking.

'Before she would answer my questions, she had to know all about how Elliot was doing and if he was getting along with his father.

' "They barely know each other, you understand," she said. "Eleanor had to leave with Elliot and Cassandra before Bill got the chance to know his son. I hope they get along. You see, my boy, I can't take care of anyone any longer. Cassandra was the last one. I simply can't manage."

' "Elliot's fine," I told her. "He's a natural mining engineer to hear his father tell it. They're working claims near Tin Cup. You don't need to worry about Elliot."

'Her mouth was dry and she signalled for me to hand her the glass of water. I did so. I asked her again how I could find Cassandra. I told her that I'd come to ask her to marry me.

' "I'm afraid you're too late," said Maureene. "She went after that John Pratt. Frankly, you seem more suitable for her than he does."

'Maureene was not certain, but she thought Cassandra had gone off somewhere into Georgia.

'I could see it now. Maureene was not tired or sick. She was dying. As if the plug in me was pulled, I could feel my energy draining out. I asked her if she minded if I sat down for a spell. I suppose I became in that moment at Maureene's bedside an older man, well beyond my twenty years and with a broken heart to boot.'

Sy paused for a moment to collect his thoughts.

'I will always remember how this fragile woman of seventy or so brought me into her bedroom and let me sit in the rocker by her bed. Before her white hand reached for mine, it fluttered on the bed covers for a moment as if to describe the path Cassandra had taken following John Pratt into Georgia.

'I took her hand. Her watery light blue eyes did not leave my face. Her thin white hair was a wisp of cloud on the pale blue pillow slip. It seemed that if I were to lift off the quilted comforter she might have floated to the ceiling. She told me with her eyes and weak smile and with the light pressure of her hand that she hoped that Cassandra would drop John Pratt and come to her senses and realize that she was all wrong for a man like that man from Georgia.

' "They seemed to get along all right while he was here at the house," she said. "He had momentary fits of stubbornness and starts of anger. He seemed able to control himself well enough. He was out of his element, of course, which I gather is the woods, his turpentine camp, the swamps over in Georgia."

'Maureene said that Cassandra would soon learn that Pratt had a taste for women, any kind of woman would do, and she hoped that Cassandra would not let herself be reduced to begging for his attention.

' "I hope I raised that young lady a few rungs above that, above crawling. Crawling will only make him turn against her and he'll become vulgar and mean. He has meanness in him," she said. "I could see that. But I don't think he is unmanly enough to hurt her."

'I leaned forward, my hands on my knees, my rumpled hat on the floor by my boot. I did not miss a word from this woman who continued to speak even as her voice grew tired, so tired now that she had to whisper. She motioned for me to bring the rocker closer still to her bedside, which I did.

'Maureene told me that I should know something first. I should know that Cassandra was carrying John Pratt's child and that she went after him because of that primarily, because she wanted to take the baby to its father.

' "That's why Cassandra ran out of Saint Charles to catch up with him," she said. "It's only because of the child. It isn't because she loves him." '

The car windows had frosted white and we both heard a pounding noise on the roof. It was Ben.

'Are you still out here? You'll freeze to death.'

'Not until Graden's car runs out of gas, we won't.'

'Don't you want some coffee. I've made a fresh pot.'

'Any word yet?

'No.'

'Coffee would be nice. You, Graden?'

'Thanks.'

Ben left us and Sy continued.

'So I was not jilted by Cassandra. After all, she had broken no promise. She had not chosen me, even though I had chosen her; she did not have me frozen in her mind, as I did her in mine. Naturally, my pride was hurt, but the wound cut deeper than that, and after my time with Maureene it became a lasting hurt. I have never stopped asking myself, "If I loved the woman, then why didn't I do something about it sooner?"

'During her last days Maureene was weak but wanted my company and asked me to wait with her. Her house was empty now except for the house servants and the nurse. She had outlived both her sister Susannah and her brother Uncle Tom. She had outlived her foster daughter Helen and outlived Helen's daughter Eleanor. The two living DuVals after Maureene were Eleanor's children, Elliot and Cassandra; and Elliot was in Denver and Cassandra was off somewhere in west Georgia. There was no one left. It was late April, nineteen twenty-nine, when Maureene DuVal died. She wanted me beside her bed. I watched her hands flutter on the coverlet like broken birds, white and fluttering, awake with memory, helpless with love.

'After Maureene's funeral, I went to find Cassandra. Her trail was cold by then — after all, she had been gone ten days by that time — but I went after her anyway, crossing western Kentucky into Tennessee. At French Lick, Georgia, I rode the woods looking for John Pratt's turpentine camp.

'It was isolated, far from even the smallest settlement, because it was a town in itself, contained and self-sufficient. All the necessaries were sold in the commissary; the women raised vegetables, pigs, chickens, and now and again, one of the men would capture a land turtle or shoot a wild hog. If I had not been on horseback the afternoon I entered a stand of slash pine about twenty-five miles southwest of French Lick, Pratt's woodsrider probably would have cut me down with his whip, taking me for a runaway. Those people did not expect or seek visitors.

'I was shown into camp, because I insisted that I tell Cassandra the news of Maureene's death myself. I hoped this would bring her back to her senses.

'Pratt's camp had a dirt track through it and ten or so buildings — no church, no school, no doctor — and was located deep in the remote woods. Shacks lined one side of the dirt track where the black workers lived. The white commissary man and his woman, Pratt and Cassandra, the woodsrider Prewitt and his wife Sally lived on the other side of the track where the sawmill, the turpentine still and the barn and wood shelter stood. That was all. It was a dingy settlement, more run-down than the mining camps that I'm used to, set as it was in a hidden, flat, swamp world with its own rules, lost from view by slash and long leaf pine. Pratt's men were drawing pine sap from the younger trees and cutting the old. Cassandra cooked, kept his house. Her best company was the commissary man's woman. That was all. In a mining camp, at least all the men stand a chance, however slim, to get rich. In Pratt's camp, only he stood that chance.'

'Here. Take it,' Ben said, passing us a Thermos and a plate of warm cookies. 'Carla's still on the phone. Eva says she's flying up here in the morning.'

'Eva. Damn,' said Sy. 'I'll be in soon.

'Anyway, I was still on my horse when I came up to her house, but Prewitt the woodsrider held the reins, leading me in like a prisoner. Of course, Cassandra recognized me. She was even glad to see me, a face from the past. But she made it known that it was awfully inconvenient of me to show up. In spite of being worn out, she was healthy. She always got healthy when she was pregnant. Also, she was planning to leave. But I didn't know that and had arrived at a bad time, a very bad time. I remember how stunned she was to see me. I must have looked a sight.

'"I can't leave," she told me. "Not yet."

'She said how kind I was to want to marry her and to come all that way just to ask, but that she was already married.

'But Cassandra was exhausted. She'd been there two months and was just plain worn out from getting used to the place. She looked healthy and glowed the way some women do when they're pregnant, but Cassandra was numb in spirit, slowed down and made drowsy and mechanical by the hard work. All of them were like that, all except for Pratt. You see, Pratt held them there

— his wife Cassandra included. They were like slaves, indentured servants, or something.

'Perhaps I had no concept, none, of what was going on. I thought I could ride in there all cocky and take her away, but it just didn't work like that. You see, she wasn't ready to leave, and most certainly did not need rescuing.

'Cassandra and I sat on the small porch of Pratt's tin-roofed shack. The stoicism of her reaction to Maureene's dying made me believe that she was sunk there, lost to me, to the rest of the world. Her hands did not shake, her eyes did not tear, her voice did not quaver. She did not invite me to stay for anything more than a cup of her poor boiled coffee. I had the impression that the woman was broken, had lost her will, her pride. Her passiveness thoroughly shocked me. She was not the same person. However, she did encourage me some by saying she could not leave "yet." She said, no, she did not need my help.

'"I'll be fine," she said. "Let me be for now."

'That was all she would hint as to her own intentions. Her lip looked like it had a fresh cut on it. I thought they were chapped. It did not occur to me, she had been kissed hard by Pratt earlier that morning and that she had returned her husband's rough kiss.

'I wasn't wanted there, it seemed, so I finished the coffee. She insisted that I leave then, giving me no sign, none, that she was unhappy there or that she was being held against her will, or that she was planning to leave on her own. She called for Prewitt the woodsrider who was nearby to escort me from the camp, so I wouldn't get lost again.

'Then she got sick — or said she was sick. In any case, her fever came to her as a blessing, at least it seems so to me, and probably it saved her life. At least it got her quit of the camp and into the town of French Lick where there was a doctor, who sent her to another doctor in a town further west, where there was a clinic where she was told that she needed a specialist who was located even further west.

'All the time she was drawing money from the account that was set up in her name at The Bank of Saint Charles. She did not expect to draw upon nor to receive any of her husband's money or his charity or his concern or his attention. She relied on her own resources for this, which succeeded in pulling her away from John Pratt. She passed from doctor to doctor until finally, as if she had been pulling herself home by a strong silver cord, hand over hand, back across Georgia and Alabama and Tennessee and into Missouri, she arrived hand over hand at the empty yellow house on Olive Street where she stayed and rested and grew strong, preparing herself to give birth to her first child, Carla's mother, May, in the front parlor, with the assistance of the same nurse who had, only months earlier, ministered to Maureene.

'May came out squalling. Such a squall of a love-child she was — earnest and eager and as hungry for life as her mother was.

'Even though Cassandra was exhausted and heartsick — remember that she was still in love — even then, she was still in love with Pratt. By the time May was born in Saint Charles, I was off in New Mexico, back to work for the cattle association on a drive far west of Albuquerque. When Cassandra and baby May could travel, she sold the big house, which had been in the family for all those years, and moved west to Denver where she lived with her half-brother Elliot. She never would have me.

'Oh hell, I wrote a song about all this, which you heard the other night.'

Sy had finished telling me his song about Cassandra, his life's most important song. Kate had told me hers about him. Now, Sy had told me his. And it felt true to me, though I didn't much like what it said.

'What do you think happened to Kate?' I asked him.

'The same thing that did to your granddad,' he said, with no hesitation.

'She killed herself?'

'Yup. You can bet on it.'

'But why? She has so much. She's popular and smart and kind. Why would she do that to herself?'

'Her mother's been trying to kill herself for years,' said Sy. 'Men. Drink. You name it. But hasn't managed it yet. Our Kate simply showed her how it's done. She's given Eva the courage.'

I put my hand on Sy's arm. 'You can't possibly mean that. She's too young. Why?'

'Wait until you know her mother a little better,' he said. 'She's a true bitch, that Eva is.'

'But, I know her mother, Sy. She's not like that. Not at all.'

'Now don't go acting like that. I let myself get that way over Cassandra and where am I? She's gone, Graden. Don't let it start eating you up. Just look here at me and you can reckon how far that kind of devotion will get you.'

He got out of the car. A gust of cold wind came off the lake ice. It was strong enough to make the aspen branches rattle. He huddled into himself against the cold. His eyes watered.

'Nineteen years old. It's a wonder the kid lasted this long,' he said. 'God knows I tried.'

With that he went back to the cabin. He looked enormous then, like a huge brown bear lumbering in the black woods. As he fought against the cold wind, his shirt sleeves flapped, ragged against his thin arms.

I cleared the windshield and drove away from the Cooke cabin and stopped for Elaine Frieze at the gate. Kate's dog Bessie did not dash out to suck exhaust or nip at the tires. The black lab was snug inside the gatehouse. When I approached, Elaine stepped outside onto the porch.

There is something about a gate, about having to stop and check in and out, that makes people feel safe somehow. In my own dreams there are gates and keepers who let the dreamer pass. This gate made me feel that I was beginning to belong here, that I was known and was welcome, that I was free to travel beyond the barrier, and free to return again, in spite of everything.

'Bessie's been keeping me company,' Elaine said. 'She's waiting to share my night-time snack.' Elaine wore a down vest over her housecoat. 'Right now my brother Elmer's gone for two weeks over at Villa Grove doing the final assessment work on his claim before the end of the year. His daughter cooks for him. Kitty's got an antique shop and fruit stand on the road out of Saguache. I hope he finishes up before it snows.'

'Elaine,' I said, 'Kate's gone missing.'

I had to yell at her. She had 'Slow Fires' playing on her tape deck. Sy's song drifted out of the small window.

'So that's who it is,' she said. 'I heard something about it on the scanner this afternoon. Our Kate. Do you hear that, Bessie? You don't suppose she's hiding out in one of the empty cabins, do you?' The dog barked happily at Elaine. 'Kate and Sy, they sure get along fine. Just like he did with her grandmother.' She waited as if she expected me to reply. When I didn't, she continued, 'Sy was devoted to Katie's grandmother, you know, but she wouldn't have him. Can you take that? I say the woman was misguided. Me, I'd take Sy in a minute.

'He treated Cassandra's daughters like he was their own father. I've always thought Cassandra's passing is what brought on his first stroke. After she died he was as lonely as I've ever seen anyone. How's Sy taking this? Pretty hard, I bet. Kate's a fine girl. Isn't she now, Bessie?' She reached to pat the dog. 'She'll show up,

Bess. She's young remember. Probably she's just run off with some guy. She'll come back.'

I was impressed, even heartened somewhat, by the gatekeeper's lack of concern.

'Those DuVal women,' Elaine continued, 'are always calling attention to themselves. Carla not so much as Kate, and of course her mother. I've known all of them — Cassandra, May, Eva, Kate — they've been traipsing in and out of here for as long as I've been in charge of this gate. One would think they're royalty by the way they act. Not Carla so much. Her dad's seen to raise her right. But those other ones ride high, not like the rest of us do. Don't misunderstand me. I feel for the girl. God forbid she's got herself in a pickle. I feel for all of them. They get under your skin after a while and you care, even if you don't approve.'

When Elaine raised the barricade, Bessie barked again and I passed by and into the darkness. Once I was on the highway I slid my copy of the Wranglers' cassette into the console.

'Slow Fires' came on. Sy's is a sad song. He calls it 'a lament for a far-ago, long-lost love which continues to burn in this old man's heart.' It is moving the way Sy sings it.

Listening to it now, here in my snow-covered cabin, makes my vision blur. For some reason, which I don't fully understand, I have got it into my head that the song is directed at me and that it is about loss and a man's life spent while asleep, that it is about my own lost time and my own lost love which cannot be recovered.

A part of the song goes:

> And when God rests Himself
> in the Rocky Mountain twilight,
> I hope one day if he's cold
> that he'll warm His hands up close
> to the slow fires

> still burning deep
> deep
> inside my heart.

I suppose I must one day accept 'Slow Fires' as my own life's song, after all, and not Helen's and Uncle Tom's.

•Sixteen•

The next morning I tried to contact the Cookes for news of Kate and the telephone went unanswered at the cabin, so I drove up the valley to Kate's trailer.

From the look of the mess inside — dishes in the sink and on the little table, the rumpled bedspread and her pillows on the floor, her scattered clothes — it looked as if she'd left abruptly, but didn't plan to be gone for long. There was fruit and salad vegetables in the ice box. Juice. Milk. Spring water. The black notebook, which holds her stories, and a box of cereal were on the table. All seemed normal, like a child's messy room. No sign of an intruder. No foul play. No note for me. It was chilly inside. She had remembered to turn down the heat when she left. She must have slept here on Monday night, the last time I saw her, and the next morning had juice and cereal for breakfast before she got Flame from the barn and went for a ride. That was twenty-four hours ago. Flame was not in the pasture or barn. The Aikins had not returned from Albuquerque.

From the trailer I went to the swim shop at Trimble looking for Carla.

There was a saloon and boarding house there in Randolph Wells's time. Now the changing stalls and huge soaking tubs have been replaced with the swim shop decorated as a sort of Bauhaus Native American health spa, with sky blue walls, turquoise counter tops, sage and brick towels, sunset and white PVC pool furniture. The pool is Olympic-sized with two small feeder pools connected by culverts. The smallest, fed by a mineral-encrusted pipe stuck in the red sandstone cliff, remains at a constant one hundred and nineteen degrees. The place was started as a health and pleasure resort and was once known throughout the mining towns in the San Juan Mountains for the curative qualities of its sulphurous water and for its female staff. No doubt my grandfather went there now and again for a soak.

Carla was at the hot pool talking to a couple of workmen who were scraping mineral deposits out of the open culvert connecting the small and middle pools.

Only two patrons, both wearing identical down jackets, sat at the edge of the hot pool, their shoes beside them, their trousers rolled up — a man and a woman, two lovers in quiet conversation. I moved a pool chair into a sunny spot some distance away to wait until Carla finished with the workmen.

Soon she approached, walking fast. Nothing needed saying on her part. She wanted, expected, news.

I avoided looking at her directly; and my eyes glancing away from her steady, anxious gaze must have told her what she suspected. There was no news. She was unable to, or didn't want to, take her eyes off me, unaware perhaps of the impression she gave to the curious workmen.

Such urgency made me feel helpless. I could do nothing. I was there to offer help and now realized that I did not know how to comfort her. I was too concerned about my own loss to be in any condition to comfort anyone.

I followed Carla into the shop. She said that Ben went to school early to collect Kate's belongings which they would store until after Christmas and then send along to Eva, if Kate did not return.

It seemed that nothing I did or said was of any comfort to her and this sent me into a senseless feeling of self blame.

She took a white terry cloth swimming robe from under the counter and made herself busy unfolding it and draping it over the shoulders of a mannequin in the window.

'It looked cold,' Carla explained.

When she looked at me again, a sign of understanding passed across her face. She had, by then, shrunk away from me, closed up into herself.

Finally, Carla spoke, 'You must forgive me. I know I seem unappreciative, but I'm worried. I'm almost certain I know what's happened. I really am. I know what's wrong. I know what's happened to her. That Kate is so much like her mother. I love Eva and all, but that's what's wrong. It makes me furious. I know Eva's behind this. She is, I know she is. This must sound like foolishness to you, but consider it for a minute. One, Kate goes after a man without knowing diddly about him. Kate is always doing that, just like her mother. Two, she is sincere. She thinks she likes these men. Three, they disappoint her because they aren't serious. They tease her and leave.'

'I hope you're wrong,' I said. 'I don't feel that way about her.'

'I know you don't. My emotions are in the way. The best way I can get clear of them is to think all the way around something. My dad taught me to do that. His father was half Navajo. You get thoughts clear of feelings by thinking about something — one single question — all the way around. First, you imagine that you are facing east, then south, then west, then north. I used to physically change positions. It's a way, a way to go about thinking. North is last, the result. That's when you lock it up and the thought is solid.'

'I understand, Carla. Please go on,' I said.

'East comes first because the sun rises, is born, in the east. Then the south, gentle and warm for growing; and then the west which is open and expansive. Finally, north, which is cold and concludes the thinking. There isn't any Navajo magic in it. It's a method. It's my way. It's what I do in order to be able to hear my heart. It's the way I decided that I knew for certain that I loved Ben. So it works for me.

'Here's how I figure what happened to Kate. Look to the east and you see the beginning, the birth which was his mystery to her. He is strange and different. He seems like a magic king to her. That's the way a man seems to any woman who is interested in him. Kate saw kingliness and was captured.'

'Maybe her feelings frightened her,' I said. 'She might be running away from them, or hiding.'

But Carla ignored that.

'Now face south,' she said. 'And you see the invitation. She accepted it. There was nothing delicate about it. She just went after him the way her mother does whenever she sees a man who appeals to her.

'Now face west. The expanse, the open, the ever-receding horizon. I think she fell in love with him, or with the idea of him. But I think he didn't care that much.

'Now face north. He wants to get out of this for some reason. He has a girl friend. It gets too sticky. Kate brings him in too deep. So he tells her something that frightens her or makes her ashamed. Or he abandons her.'

Suddenly I was cold, almost shaking. An almost

ghostly figure of a beautiful girl, a lost girl, entered my blurred vision. How could Carla be so certain about what had happened to Kate? So positive? Hers was a most horrible kind of prophecy.

'Sy won't talk about her,' Carla said. 'He's frozen up. I think he's blaming Eva for this, too.'

I did not tell Carla what Sy had said about Kate and suicide the night before. I still wasn't certain he was right. Besides, I thought, anything, even Carla's theory of what had happened, was better than Sy Cooke's.

I left Carla then. Disoriented, purposeless, I was frightened for Kate. I had not abandoned her.

First I went to Ben's office at the college and learned that he was meeting with the sheriff. At Sheriff Connor's office on Second Avenue, I was taken to a conference room. Ben and five of Kate's friends were seated at a conference table. The room would not hold enough chairs, so I stood in the open doorway. It was airless and close in the room.

The sheriff sat at the table's head and asked each student to try and remember anything, the smallest detail about the last time each of them had seen Kate, anything at all, however insignificant a detail it might seem. 'We believe she's missing,' he said, 'and we have no evidence of foul play. Now, each of us has a picture in his mind about what might have happened, what went on. I would like to be able to ask you to forget those pictures, but I can't. We don't have much to go on, so I must ask you to come forward and tell me what you can.' The sheriff looked at each of them. 'When did you last see her?'

'In class on Friday,' said Billy Hinkle, 'in Doctor Cooke's class.'

'She was in class,' said Ben. 'I haven't seen her since.'

'Neither have I,' said Steve.

'We went to The One Note first on Saturday night,'

said a girl called Frances. 'She wasn't there. Then I saw her in The Barrel later on.'

'I knew she was going there,' said Sarah McCall, Kate's room-mate. 'A bunch of us went later and saw her with a man. I recognized him, sort of, but I don't know who he is.'

'What does he look like?'

'He was older,' said a girl called Betty. 'A skier, I think.'

'How old?'

'I can't tell. Maybe as old as Doctor Cooke. Maybe even thirty,' said Sarah McCall.

'I'm thirty,' said Ben.

'Your age,' said Sarah McCall, 'but he had longer hair and wore a cowboy hat and a white shirt with pearl-snap buttons. I remember that. He looked neat. I would have gone out with him.'

'Did he pick Kate up? Was she on a date?' the sheriff asked Sarah McCall.

'No. She left our room about six-thirty. I don't know how she got to town. A ride, probably. It's no problem to get a ride. When Frances and Betty and I got there, Katie was with this man.'

'That's it,' said Frances. 'They were off to them-selves.'

'She gets snobby at times,' said Betty, 'like we're too young for her. She ignored us. She definitely wanted to be alone with that guy.'

'A hunk,' said Frances, 'to keep for herself. I think he works in a gas station in Bayfield. Maybe. I'm not sure.'

'Really,' said Betty. 'A hunk.'

'I think he was a surfer or a skier,' said Frances.

'What about the guy who runs the laundromat?' asked Betty. 'He was a super-hunk.'

'She's not seeing him anymore,' said Sarah McCall. 'He has a wife. Boy, that really got her when she found out. He hid his ring on her.'

'Do you have a name?' asked the sheriff.

'Price Jones,' I said. 'He's at the Las Animas Laundry out by Trimble.'

It seemed that by now the students had shifted their interest away from Kate slightly — though not entirely. The emotions which ran so high after Tuesday's assembly had less voltage this morning. No doubt, once the students and faculty became immersed in the upcoming exams and the future Christmas break, the tragedy which struck the DuVal family became a rather vague event in their lives.

'Now, tell me what you can about this ski bum,' said the sheriff, after putting down Jones's name on his little pad.

'I went over to their table,' said Sarah McCall, 'to ask her if she wanted a ride.'

'What time was that approximately?'

'Almost twelve,' said Frances. 'I remember looking at Betty's watch. We have to be back at the dorm by twelve-thirty on weekends.'

'I hate that,' said Steve. 'What are we, children? I can stay out as late as I want at home.'

'Just check out with the RA and you can,' said Betty. 'That's what I do.'

'Did Kate check out?' asked Sheriff Connor.

'No. Not that I know of,' said Ben.

'Anyway,' said Sarah McCall, 'I went to their table, Sheriff, and asked Katie if she wanted a ride. She gave me this look.'

'Look? What look?'

'Yeah, like "Go away. I've got something going here." She liked the guy. Then she did this strange thing. She pushed her stuff toward me. Her purse and watch. And she took off the Indian necklace she wears and told me to take it and to cover for her at the dorm.'

'Did she say why she was giving you her identification?'

'No. I just did what she wanted. I thought, well, I guess I thought that when you're going swimming, you usually take off your watch. No, I didn't need to ask her why. It was a little strange, but I did it for her. All the time the guy smiled at me. He was a little drunk, so his smile was happy and sort of goofy.'

'So you took her personal effects back to the school and you covered for her?'

'Yes. On Saturday night. When I didn't see her on Sunday or all day Monday, I got worried. So, yesterday afternoon I went to the office and told them I didn't know where she was.'

'What else do you remember?'

'There is one other thing,' said Sarah McCall. 'Kate moved her hand away from her drink and put it under the table onto his leg. Not just on his knee, Sheriff, you know?'

'That's Kate,' said Frances. 'She can get away with that.'

'You covered for her from Saturday night until Tuesday afternoon?'

'Kate is Kate,' Sarah McCall said to the sheriff, snapping at him now. 'Sometimes she stays out all night. If I'd been worried, I would have called Doctor Cooke, she's his cousin. Besides, she's done it before, but not for so long.'

'By marriage,' said Ben. 'She's my cousin by marriage.'

'But I wasn't worried,' said Sarah McCall. 'There wasn't any reason to worry. She wanted to be with that guy. I could tell that. You have to know her. She knows more about men than some of the rest of us do.'

'She knows how to manage them. I'll say that,' said Betty. 'She's had about five boyfriends since school started. One right after the other.'

'Not that many,' said Frances. 'Maybe three.'

'Kate is not a trouble maker,' said Ben. 'She sticks out and can be stubborn. She likes excitement.'

'What more can you tell me about her?'

'Kate is just Kate,' said Frances. 'What's to tell?'

'She's too sweet,' Betty said. 'And she's no good at

chemistry. I'm her lab partner.'

'She smart,' said Billy Hinkle, 'real smart. A neat woman.'

'She has a chance for honors in English,' said Ben.

'A little wild,' said Frances.

'Yes. She's always ready for a party. But not a party girl. If you know what I'm saying,' Betty said.

'What's that?'

'She plays. But she isn't a big drinker or a lush. She isn't an alcoholic or anything.'

'I think she's awesome,' said Steve.

'Get real, Steve. She doesn't know you exist,' said Billy.

'She's a good student,' said Ben. 'One of the best I've had.'

'Not like that,' Steve said to Billy. 'I like her, man. We're friends. We have these great talks.'

'Was she depressed or unhappy about anything?'

'Not really,' said Sarah. 'She was ready to go skiing with some of us over Christmas. She does get homesick sometimes.'

'We all do,' said Frances, 'sometimes.'

'Not that often,' said Steve, 'except when I'm broke.'

'She doesn't have a regular boyfriend?' asked the sheriff.

'Not anymore,' said Steve, looking over his shoulder at me 'She did for a while.'

'I can't say for sure,' said Sarah McCall. 'She's private about that.'

'None that we know of,' said Ben. 'Not recently.'

I kept quiet. My heart was pounding.

'She's never said anything to me,' said Betty.

'I think she likes to play the field,' said Sarah.

'I went out with her,' said Billy Hinkle, 'for brunch.'

'You?' said Frances.

'Like for a McDonalds,' said Steve.

'In case you're interested, they let Indians in the Strater,' said Billy Hinkle. 'I took her two Sundays ago for German waffles and roast beef.'

'What makes you so certain that she's missing?' asked the sheriff.

'She's been gone too long,' said Sarah. 'She's never been gone this long before.'

They all seemed to agree on that point.

Sheriff Connor assured them that he would begin missing persons procedures, regardless of how the college handled the case. This seemed to relieve the group. The sheriff stood now and adjusted his hat and holster. Steve, Billy Hinkle, Frances and Betty thanked Sheriff Connor and left the small room.

Outside a basketball player was waiting. He was dressed in his practice uniform and warm-ups. He approached Ben, Sarah McCall and the sheriff.

The center for the Fort Lewis Nuggets, John Stetson, a bit chagrined, admitted to them that he was out after curfew on Saturday night and that he had seen Kate leave The Barrel about one in the morning, Sunday morning, with a man wearing a white shirt and a cowboy hat. Stetson said he had watched the couple walk down Main which was empty at that hour and drive away in a white truck.

'I think it was a Ford,' he said. 'It might have had a silver camper top. I'm not sure. I remember thinking that Katie must be really heated because she had this Levi jacket on over her shoulders. No parka.'

'Are you sure it was Kate DuVal?'

'Yes, sir. I know her.'

'Do you know who she was with?'

'No. He wasn't from school. I'm pretty sure about that.'

'Is this the guy here?' the sheriff asked, pointing at me.

'No, sir. I've seen them together. But not for a while.'

The sheriff cautioned the ball player about staying in training and a much relieved John Stetson excused himself.

'I wasn't really worried until Tuesday,' said Sarah

McCall. 'She usually tells me when she isn't coming home or calls to check in the morning. It wasn't that she spent the night with someone. What bothers me is that she gave me her purse and stuff. I can't explain that part. Then I think how she put her hand on him. Anyway, I didn't get even a little bit worried until Carla, Mrs. Cooke, called yesterday while I was in the room typing my history paper. I said Kate wasn't there, but I didn't say she hadn't come home yet.' Sarah McCall now spoke to Ben. 'I'm sorry I didn't say anything about that, Doctor Cooke. But I wasn't worried. She stayed out for two or three nights a lot of times. I always cover for her.'

'If you have time,' the sheriff said to Ben, 'I'd like to talk to the bartender. We're finished with you for now, young lady.'

'I'm getting some flyers printed,' Sarah said. 'We're going to put them up all over campus and in all the businesses.'

'I'll take some when they're ready,' said Ben.

'Post them wherever she might have been,' said the sheriff.

I left my car where it was on Third Avenue and got into Ben's van. We followed the sheriff to The Barrel on Main next to the train depot.

Inside Ned was eating lunch. When he saw Sheriff Connor, he wiped his mustache and got off the bar stool.

He shook hands with Ben.

'What's the trouble, Sheriff?'

'Ned,' said Ben. 'Kate's gone. Have you seen her?'

'Kate?' said Ned.

'She was seen here on Saturday with a guy in a cowboy hat,' said the sheriff, 'a skier type.'

'We get lots of students in here, Sheriff. Do we have an ID problem?'

'I don't, if you don't, Ned. The girl was here real late last Saturday. Tall, dark hair, pretty, distinguished nose, dark eyes.'

'Blue,' I said. 'They look dark, but they're actually blue.'

'Oh, that's Katie,' said Ned. 'Yeah, she was here Saturday. She's in a lot, usually with two or three friends. I haven't seen her this week, so far.' He spoke to me. 'She's a friend of yours, Graden, isn't she?'

'She is,' I said.

'Do you know who she was with on Saturday?' the sheriff asked Ned.

'He's new. Comes in once in a while, but I don't know who he is. A long-haired guy. Quiet. I'd recognize him again. Probably an out-of-towner. I've seen Kate with him lately. She's left with him a few times.'

Ned bit off a chunk of pickle.

'You're sure it was Kate, Kate DuVal?'

'I know Kate. Not her last name. I don't know anybody's last name, Sheriff. She came in about ten-thirty or eleven, and sat at the bar with a pitcher of Sunrises. Not beer. She doesn't like beer. Then this long-hair ski-bum type comes in and after a while I see she's with him over at that table in the corner. It was a busy night. It always is before finals. I sort of lost track of her in the crowd.'

'Did she leave with the long-hair?'

'About one, one-thirty. They left together. I closed right after that. I remember they were the last ones to go.'

'Did you see anything peculiar?'

'Not really. They stayed at that same table, and Connie took them drinks. Maybe they danced a few times. Went to the john.'

'What else?'

'She wasn't wearing a coat. It was cold out. When they left, he put his Levi jacket over her shoulders. He had on a white shirt, real white and starched. A friendly guy. He put a ten in the tip glass.'

'Was she drunk?'

'Not really. High. Laughing. Happy. That's all. Kate

doesn't get drunk.'

'Did they speak to anyone else?'

'I don't think so. They were by themselves. Well, one of her friends did go over to them. But that's all I saw. It was crowded in here. Sheriff, she's in here all the time.'

We left Ned to his lunch. Outside The Barrel, Sheriff Connor suggested that Ben call Eva.

'She's probably on her way here now,' I said. 'She's flying in this morning sometime.'

'That's just as well. The girl won't go home. If that was her plan, she'd be there by this time. Don't tell her mother that. Just say we've started looking. I'll begin at the Aikins' place.'

'She's not there, Sheriff,' I said. 'I went by first thing this morning. The horse is gone, too. You might check the laundromat. Price Jones might have seen her leave.'

He seemed to ignore my suggestion and asked Ben to search the northeast section of the county over by the Vallecito Reservoir, checking the campgrounds at Pine Point and North Canyon, the ones on Graham and Old Gardeners creeks, and then to loop south over the Grassy Mountains into Bayfield and Gem Village.

'It's a long shot,' said the sheriff. 'You're looking for an ordinary white truck with a cap and a couple of love birds in it. The guy thinks he's a cowboy. There are plenty of those out there. Check the gas stations, too.'

'What can I do?' I asked.

'Stay with him,' said the sheriff. 'And keep in touch.'

Ben kindly asked me to drive along with him to help watch the side roads and to search the campgrounds.

We have plenty of snow here now, it came late to the La Plata Mountains, this winter, but dust was still on the road to Vallecito reservoir, filming slick ice patches. Ben and I spotted few white Ford trucks. Only one at Old Gardeners Creek campground had a silver camper top. I spoke to the owner, an old woman wrapped in a sleeping bag. Her son was out on the ice fishing with salmon eggs. She said they were from Tucson and had been at the site for ten days. She had not seen another truck like theirs.

At one point during the drive, I wondered if Kate might be hiding at my cabin. A long shot to say the least, given the distance and the cold. Still, the place was snug, plenty of fire wood. One could easily survive there. Access could be had from the lake or from U.S. 550.

'We'd see smoke,' Ben said. 'It hangs low on these cold days and builds up when there's no wind. From the smoke you can see who's in residence at any cabin. This morning we saw no smoke up the lake. The Eastmans, the Carvers, the Boones — no smoke. Bob Adams', the caretaker's had smoke. A fireplace puts out lots and lots of it, and steam. You'd see it as a haze.'

'My woodstove is air-tight,' I said, 'and doesn't put out that much smoke. And, Ben, my cabin is at least two miles from yours. Maybe the wind was blowing up there.'

'I don't think so,' he said.

So I let that possibility drop until the next morning. I let it drop for too long.

Circling back west to Durango, we went through Bayfield, a small town that resembles a New England village in a grove of cottonwood trees and willows on the Los Pinos river, and through Gem Village, a town built on the highway with shops selling rare rocks and a cafe made from oil barrels, and passed under the lip of Carbon Mountain, 'walking mountain' which rests on a stratum of shale. Water seeping into the shale formation greases the sandstone above, causing the mountain to move a few millimeters east each year. We saw no more white Ford trucks. It was just above freezing.

•SEVENTEEN•

It was dark by the time Ben dropped me off at my car. I stopped by The Barrel. Ned had nothing new. I ate at the Thunderbird Cafe on Main and afterwards went directly to my room. I was in bed before eleven. There was nothing about Kate on the late news. By that time the temperature had dropped to twenty above zero with clear skies and winds at fifteen to twenty knots from the north-northeast.

In the morning, I put on warm clothes and called Sy, asking him to arrange for his friend Bob Adams, the lake's caretaker, to run me up the lake over the ice on his snowmobile to my cabin. Sy thought I was foolish, but I had to confirm one way or the other what I suspected. I was convinced that Kate's ancestors had taken her into the woods at the north end of the lake where she was waiting for me; what Mrs.

Aikin had said still lingered severely and had me in an agony of anticipation. Kate was fond of me, Mrs. Aikin said, and that could only mean she wanted to be with me, that she had gone looking for me after all. And I thought I knew right where she was. Safe and snug in my cabin, having ridden the ten miles on Flame.

Sy agreed to call Adams, and with those arrangements made, I left the motel, expecting that the snowmobile would be waiting for me when I got there, and began to drive up the valley to the lake. But it was on the way there, just as the sun came over the east ridge, not far from the main house at the Simpson Ranch on the S-curve of U.S. 550, that I spotted, grazing in an open field, Aikin's roan.

I pulled off the highway near the narrow gauge tracks and found that the fence along the road to the Simpson's south pasture was cut. The sun was still low. It was cold in the pasture with the wind whipping down the valley from the north. Flame spotted me and immediately came towards me, expecting carrots. I had nothing for him to eat, but held out my hand as if I did, and the roan waited for me at the cut fence and then went up the hillside. Before I went after him, I repaired the fence so he wouldn't bolt onto the highway; using my belt and handkerchief, I was able to splice the two top wires fairly tight. Near a fence post I found a pair of wire cutters. A trail of broken weeds led off toward the cliffs where Flame now stood waiting for me. From the frozen horse tracks and footprints, it looked as if someone had led the horse to the fence, cut it, mounted up again, heading north following the railroad tracks into the gorge and on up the canyon to the old stagecoach road which follows Elbert creek up to Haviland lake and on to Electra.

I knew what I was going to find at the upper end of the pasture at the base of the cliffs there and walked slowly across the frozen ground toward Flame, who stood waiting not far from a pile of rocks. Then I saw her. She was lying face down in the high grass, her head resting on a blood-smeared rock. Her neck looked broken. My voice echoed against the high rock walls as I turned her over. Her cheekbone was crushed. The sun had not yet reached her body, which was dusted with a light coating of frost. I could not stop myself from taking her into my arms, from covering her stiff, cold lips with mine.

I barely remember leaving her there, of turning off the road at the highway camp where I called Sheriff Connor. He said that he would pick up Kate's mother at the Strater and bring her to identify the body. As I was leaving, I heard his voice on the camp's police radio, reporting the location of the missing girl, calling for an ambulance, as if that would do any good now.

Elaine Frieze was not at the gatehouse, so I broke in through the back porch and called the Cookes. The line was busy or off the hook.

Elaine had the barricade down, blocking the road, so I ducked underneath the bar and ran up the road toward the Cookes'.

The winter sun was full strength now above the red cliffs; bright and harsh, turning the frozen lake into a sheet of shimmering black ice. It was cold in the sun, even out of the wind. As I ran, the air bit at my throat, punishing my lungs.

I had to find Sy. The news was horrible. Someone had to tell him in person.

The Cooke van was stopped a short distance down the road. There he was huddled in the cold shadows changing a tire. I was out of breath and could not speak immediately.

'I found her!' I said, 'It's Kate.'

Sy stopped struggling with the spare. He had not heard me.

Before I could say more, Elaine came hurrying toward us. A sudden wind whipped up the road just then, a cat's paw from off the frozen lake, thrusting Elaine forward. The dust in the air caught the tear streaks on her face leaving marks like deep brown scratches.

'Bob Adams and I heard on his scanner,' Elaine said. 'They found a girl. Probably it's not Kate. The sheriff would have called or ridden up here himself.'

Sy, unable to hold back a flash of anger, said, 'Everybody knows! Everybody, God damn, knows everything, but me.'

When Elaine saw the anger register on Sy's face, she said quickly, 'I was up seeing Bob Adams about Elmer when we heard. Elmer's in the hospital again over in Salida. His ulcer's started bleeding on him.'

'Elaine,' said Sy, quietly, releasing the jack, 'I'm very sorry about your brother. You know that. Elmer's a good friend. Now, God damn it, tell me what you heard.' He was trying to ask it softly, calmly, but it came out cold, almost mean.

A wall rose between Elaine and Sy.

'They found a girl,' Elaine told him. 'A girl's body in the pasture down at the Simpson Ranch. They didn't give out the name.'

'It's Kate, I'm afraid,' I said. 'I'm the one who called Sheriff Connor.'

'You?' said Sy.

'On my way up here I saw a horse loose,' I said. 'Flame, the Aikins' horse. When I stopped and tried to catch him so he wouldn't get out in the road, I saw something white, a blouse. There was a woman lying in the shadows in the grass. I went up to see if I could help. It was Kate, Sy. She was frozen.'

'Are you sure? Did you see her face?'

'I've just come from there, Sy.'

'Did you touch her?' Sy asked. 'Did she move?'

'No, she didn't.'

'Are you sure it's Katie?' he asked me again.

'I'm positive, Sy. I've seen her, held her in my arms.'

Elaine stood in her boots and down vest and house-coat, shifting from one foot to the other.

'Won't you get inside,' said Sy, 'out of the wind?'

I opened the van's door for her. She hesitated.

'Get in, Elaine,' Sy said. 'We'll drive you home. You can't stand out here. It's too cold.'

We finished changing his tire and tossed the tools in the back with the flat.

As Sy slammed blindly through a series of potholes, Elaine said, 'You get that tire fixed before you do anything else.'

There were two cars full of ice fishermen waiting for her at the gatehouse.

'I was supposed to open up fifteen minutes ago.' To me, she said, 'I hope that wasn't Katie you found, after all.'

We waited for her to open the gate, overhearing what she said to the men in the second car as she gave them a fishing permit.

'We have an emergency here. So fish fifteen minutes after dark if you want.' Then she padded back through the cold and dust to the van, mumbling to herself. 'I hope they all freeze their butts off.'

Suddenly, there wasn't anything more to be said.

Elaine raised the barricade for us.

'The sheriff is on his way up,' I said quietly. 'I don't know anything more. Eva's in town. He's getting her to identify the body.'

Sy hesitated, taking his hands off the steering wheel and covering his face.

'Damn Eva,' he said.

I asked him if he wanted me to take my car.

He shook his head. 'I'll get us down there.' To Elaine, he said, 'Will you please call the kids. Tell them to meet me at the Simpson Ranch. The sheriff's probably there by now.'

We lurched off, fishtailing. A brief spat of gravel hit the gatehouse, as Elaine retreated inside, presumably to telephone Carla at the cabin.

Eva was waiting alone in the sheriff's car. She was dressed in tight black ski pants and a black fur coat and black scarf and boots, all black. She saw us and climbed out of the car. In silence, we approached Sheriff Connor's men who were grouped around Kate's fallen body.

The sheriff put his hand on Eva's arm and she pulled away as if she had been shocked.

'Don't you touch me!' she shouted.

She ran directly to her daughter who was covered with a blanket. After a moment, she nodded to a deputy who slowly folded back the covering exposing the face.

Eva turned away, nodding blindly, holding out her hands. They were fluttering like frightened birds, and as I took hold of them and led her away, I could not help but think of dying Maurcene DuVal's fluttering hands, long ago in St. Charles when Sy was searching for Cassandra.

The wind in the shade of the cliff was bitter cold.

The sheriff followed us back to his car.

'We think,' Sheriff Connor said, 'that whoever was carrying her cut the fence. He planned to dispose of her at the far end of the pasture. But the hillside got too steep and she was too heavy to carry that far. So he tossed her down and dragged her a ways, rolled her over into the scrub, and left. She's been here a day, maybe two. That's just a guess.'

Eva turned and faced the sheriff. Fiercely, she told him to keep quiet. Before climbing back inside the patrol car, she stood a moment, looking back at her daughter, her broken daughter.

'I know who did it,' she said to me. 'I know who's to blame. Oh, it's not you, Graden. It's me. I am. Blame me. Not yourself or her.'

With some difficulty, I helped her into the back seat out of the bitter wind.

Sy went to her. He forced a smile.

'We can't blame you, Eva,' he said. 'You did what you thought was best. But Eva, why in God's name did you let her run loose like that? It was too much for her.' Then his voice turned mean, angry. He tried to cut himself off, but couldn't. 'She was a better rider than to let that fat roan get away from her. She let it happen. She wanted it to happen.'

I am not certain if Eva heard him or not. But she did not respond, and Sy said nothing to her after that. Those were the only words he spoke to Eva. For all I know, he has not spoken to her since.

We left Eva huddled in the sheriff's car and I suggested to the sheriff that, perhaps, Kate was thrown from the horse and not dragged to the spot.

'She liked to ride, after all, very much,' I said. 'More than anything, almost. I called you as soon as I found her. That's Joe Aikin's roan. Kate took care of it for him.'

'Possibly, you're right,' he said. 'Possibly, you did call as soon as you could. And possibly, she was raped and left to die. How else do you explain what she was doing all the way up here?'

'I believe she was looking for me,' I said. 'I have a cabin three or four miles from here. She was going there. I'm quite sure of it.'

'She can't very well tell us that, now, can she?' he said. 'You'll be around?'

'I'm staying at the Silver Spur,' I said. 'My room is paid up for a week. I'll stay longer if you need me, of course.'

The sheriff refused my proffered hand. 'Of course, you will,' he said. Before turning to other matters, he added, 'By the way, what makes you think that girl would ride this far in the cold for someone like you?'

*

By this time, Ben and Carla had arrived. We all gathered around the patrol car. The sheriff told us, just as he had told the students in his office, that it was best not to dwell on the pictures we now had in our minds. 'Instead, please, try and think of something, anything, that might help me find who did this,' and then he tapped on the window and said loudly to Eva, 'I would like to talk to you about pressing charges, at least rape charges, Ma'am.'

'She was not raped,' said Eva, coldly. 'She was not killed. I know it.'

Ben put his arm around Carla.

Sy moved away from the sheriff, his face ashen, and he soon went to Carla's car where he got into the back and waited to be driven home.

The ambulance and fire truck arrived at the same time and drove into the pasture. Kate's body was moved onto a stretcher. She was sheathed in black rubber.

Carla spoke briefly with Ben and drove out of the pasture with Sy sitting erect in the back seat. He and Carla were on their way back to the cabin.

Eva declined a ride to town with the sheriff, who said he would be by to see her later at the hotel. She got into the van with Ben and me and we slowly followed the ambulance into town.

In front of the hotel, I helped Eva climb down from the passenger's seat.

'Will you come up? Just for a while?' she asked me.

'Of course,' I said, 'certainly.'

'Ben will want to get back.'

'I'm sorry, Eva,' said Ben. 'We loved her. We all did. Very much.'

'Take care of the service for me, Ben, will you? I can't manage it. I don't know who to call.'

She was shaking. She reached for my hand, and I put my arm around her and we stood there until Ben drove away up Eighth Street.

•EIGHTEEN•

In her room, Eva poured a glass of vodka. At first she was silent, withdrawn. She swallowed mechanically, one glassful and then a second. She did not want to be comforted or contradicted. Her blue eyes were clear and sharp, sharp with anger.

'I didn't know any other way, and neither did Katie,' she said. 'I'm the one who taught her. I taught her the only way I know.'

We waited for the sheriff. She still wore her black pants and black fur coat and wanted the windows left open. When the sheriff knocked, she gripped my arm.

'I don't want to talk to him.'

As I was opening the door, she lurched forward and took my hand off the safety chain, grabbing it to balance herself. She would not let me open the door for him.

'I have to ask you again, Missus DuVal,' Sheriff Conner said. 'Will you press charges?'

'Nobody did anything wrong. Just leave me alone.' Then she slowly pushed the door all the way closed and threw the bolt.

'Do you want to be alone?' I asked Eva. 'Should I leave?'

She shook her head and hurried into the bathroom.

I heard sobbing and went to the door, calling to her. Her cries echoed from the bathroom. 'There's nothing to be done.' She was yelling it now. 'Nothing. Nothing. Damn her!'

No confrontation, no confession or arrest, no trial or sentence or act of revenge would bring Eva to the closure of her mourning. Eva could do nothing but blame herself for as long as it took her, finally, to shift the blame away from everything and everyone, so she could call Kate's death what I must now believe it to be: an accidental suicide — a willed accident — caused because I, the man she loved, had broken up with her; caused because the horse shied at ice or a white paper scrap or a pheasant clamoring skyward from the bush, and she did not bother to control the animal when she could have; caused because she was lost, alone and hurt and did not care anymore.

In the end, there was no one there to help her when she needed it. The shadows of her family were gone. Maureene DuVal could no longer offer shelter; Uncle Tom could no longer offer her love and comfort; and Sy had not been there to cling to, as he had always been for Cassandra. Kate was left — abandoned, hurt, withdrawn. All this time Eva believed that her daughter was happy at school and safe, and Ben and Carla believed that too. Only Sy understood, but he had not been there to help her. And I was not there, when I should have been.

Soon Eva came out of the bathroom. Never in my life have I witnessed such pain, not in anyone. It cut through her flesh, lacerating her face.

She howled at me. Her tears literally burned her cheeks. She pulled at her clothes and short hair as if she were on fire with grief.

The coroner would prove that the sheriff was correct about the length of time the body had lain there. Because of the cold, the skin was discolored only slightly with little sign of deterioration. The slight wounds at the wrists were recently inflicted as the clots were fresh. She had lost a shoe. Kate's ruined face was still alive-looking, as if she were sleeping there on the sharp rock. One might have thought she was doing just that, if it were not below freezing out in that wind and if her cheek were not crushed and if the grass were not a frozen spiked bed.

It did not come out, officially, until the following week that Kate probably rode the horse from Aikin's pasture, following the railroad tracks, and was thrown onto the ground and died there at the Simpson Ranch from either the neck injury or exposure. Skid tracks were found close to her, tracks made by a horse. The wire cutters had her fingerprints on them. Horse hair was under her nails and stuck to the front of her blouse and between her legs. The hair matched that of Flame, Joe Aikin's animal. The crushed cheek and the bruises on Kate's shoulders and buttocks and arms and across her breasts were made when she fell, as were the marks and slight cuts at her ankles and wrists, not because she had been in a struggle. Kate had carried the wire cutters with her from Joe Aikin's place.

She had been missing five days, and it appeared that

she was alive for at least the first three. She was not murdered, as Eva knew, not strictly speaking, but it appeared that she had willingly exposed herself to the horse and to the cold and that was what killed her. No one had seen Kate on horseback or heard her yell or seen her fall. No one had seen a girl on a horse, on Joe Aikin's roan gelding. No neighbors. No witnesses. The mute horse was the only witness.

Joe Aikin and his wife had left for Albuquerque the morning she disappeared and did not return until after the weekend. His sister's husband was looking after their place, checking the house and the gelding every day or so, and was instructed by Aikin not to worry about the roan too much unless it snowed, not to worry about hay or oats, as Kate would take care of that. The brother-in-law said that he had not checked on the horse more than twice and had done that by riding by in his truck. Flame was there on Monday morning and was missing on Thursday morning, this morning, but he didn't think much about it, knowing that Kate exercised the animal.

She died on Tuesday morning, December 13th, just before noon.

I was outside Bloomfield when she died, at a roadside cafe eating a tamale plate with green chili sauce. A short time before that, the trout had risen to take the fly.

Eva returned to the bathroom and changed out of her black clothes and put on her robe.

She said that she had had a visit from Katie's soul on Tuesday, moments, it turned out, after she died.

'I thought it was just a visit. Kate sometimes did that,' she said. 'Her spirit would visit me. We didn't write letters, so . . . But, that day, I woke from a nap and my neck hurt. That's when I knew. . . .'

Kate had lain exposed on the frozen ground for two

nights. The autopsy told of no recent sexual activity. There had been no violent struggle. She was thrown from Flame, or she fell and broke her neck.

Eva knew that. She knew her daughter.

She went over and over it. Repeating what happened. Detail by detail.

I told her that I had left Kate in her yellow trailer, that she had broken up with me, for good this time, but that she must have had second thoughts and gone searching for me, riding the horse because it was too far to walk to my cabin. She had gotten as far as the pasture on the S-curve by the Simpson Ranch when she was thrown or fell and then the cold set in. She was less than four miles from my cabin when it happened.

By early that Thursday afternoon Doctor Preston had signed the death certificate which stated the cause of death to be accidental — 'Victim was killed when thrown from a horse.'

Kate rode the horse to find me simply because the winter sun was harsh and blazing on Tuesday morning. She rode without a bridle or a saddle, using only the hackamore, because she always rode that way. Perhaps she did not know the roan well enough. It shied at its own shadow.

Kate had felt the animal's strength between her legs and the wind and the rhythm of the animal under her. There is no evil in that. There is only accident.

'There's nothing to be done. Nothing,' Eva howled, panting for breath.

At last, she reached out and accepted my hands in hers. Gradually, she became somewhat calmer, heaving with sobs, cringing, telling me that she held no desire for revenge, had no desire to blame me, held no anger against the beautiful horse or against me, and grieved only at the splendid possibilities which for her child were now lost.

Finally Eva was exhausted and we were able to sit for three or four minutes before her entire body suddenly recoiled as if lashed with a whip. Her nails dug into my hands. Afterwards she relaxed her grip and breathed deeply, gathering strength, waiting for the next surge of pain, which was so severe that each one left her shuddering weak and breathless.

•Nineteen•

The following morning it still hadn't snowed. Usually waist-deep snow covers the ground in mid-December, yet the ground was bare and frozen hard for six inches. The gravediggers would need jackhammers first and then a backhoe for Kate's grave at Greenmount Cemetery. Ben would drive to town that morning and meet with the caretaker at the cemetery and arrange for the practical matters — to get the hole dug. He had chosen the coffin and Eva had signed the papers. They would need an awning and a carpet graveside. Plywood to cover the hole in case it snowed before the service. No flowers. A grave stone.

A few hours before Kate's funeral, Sherrif Connor reached me at the Silver Spur and told me to stop by his office.

'There's something in the autopsy you should know

about,' he said. 'You two were close, yes?'

I found him waiting for me. He was sitting at his desk and did not stand when I came forward. Instead, he tapped a file on his desk in front of him.

'It seems the girl was pregnant,' he said, 'about two months gone.' His voice was cold and judgmental. He waited for that to sink in. Then he said, 'You knew all about that, of course.'

'No, I didn't,' I said. 'She hadn't told me. Not yet.'

'You would have been the father, then?'

'As far as I know. I mean, yes. I was seeing her then.'

'Well,' he said, handing me Kate's file. 'Do you want to read this?'

'That won't be necessary, Sheriff.'

He took the file back.

I held on to the back of the chair in front of his desk, anxious to leave the hot, smoke-filled room. The sheriff, instead of standing to see me out, put his feet on his desk and looked at me from under the brim of his hat.

'It happens,' he said. 'It's always a shame when it does. By the way, that ski-bum she'd been seen with. He didn't have anything to do with this.

'The white Ford truck he was driving belongs to a rancher in Bayfield. I've had him locked up since last week.'

I managed to thank him before I fled the place and went blindly down the hill off Second Street to Main. At first I could not remember where Eva was staying. Why hadn't Kate told me sooner? Why? Why had she run, run with my unborn child?

At the hotel, I took the cage and went to Eva's room. It was impossible for me to keep this to myself. I could not live with it alone. Kate's child, my child had died with her. Eva should know this — a mother would want to know such a thing, to be told, to be told by the father. I had to unburden myself.

But when she opened the door and I saw the grief-scarred face, I could not tell her.

'What's wrong?' she asked. 'You look like you've been hit by something.'

'I get waves of missing her,' I said. 'One swept over me on the way up here just now.' Then I found myself holding out my arms. I buried my face in her neck. 'Oh, Eva. You look so much like her. It will be all right.'

I had not wept for Kate, but did so now and felt like a child in Eva's arms. Yet, I could not tell her. I could never tell her. And I have not breathed a word of this to anyone until now.

•Twenty•

The burial service was at three o'clock.

Eva was ready to go by two, and I found her sitting in the room smoking. She had not touched her lunch tray.

We were waiting together when Kate's room-mate called.

'I saw about Kate in the paper here this morning,' Sarah said. 'She's on the front page.'

I covered the mouthpiece. 'It's Katie's room-mate.' Then I spoke again to Sarah. 'Eva's not taking any calls.'

'I probably should have mentioned it,' Sarah was saying, 'I just didn't.'

'What is it, Sarah?'

'I wanted to tell her that I have one of Kate's skirts, her dark green one, that I packed by mistake, and I don't know what to do with it. I mean, she let me borrow it, but now I can't think of, of what I should do with it. I have her silver and turquoise necklace, too. Should I send them?'

I still have Kate's stories here with me and am following the advice I then gave to Sarah McCall, that is to wait a time before returning them to Eva.

'What sort of necklace?'

Sarah went on to describe the silver squash blossom, the one which Eva had bought on impulse the day she saw Sean Delaney on the street with his wife and children. 'I thought, you know, it would get lost or something. Katie liked that necklace. She always wore it. I think her mother gave it to her.'

'Why don't you put it away for now with the skirt. I'm sure that Kate would want you to care for them, Sarah. Don't send them to Eva. Not just yet.'

I told Sarah that the burial service would take place that afternoon and that a memorial service would no doubt be held by the college after Christmas break. Though she lived only an hour away in Cortez, I encouraged Sarah to stay home, saying that the burial service was to be held immediately because Kate's mother wanted it over with.

'It's primarily for the family, so don't feel you must be here.'

Then I went down in the cage to the front desk and asked them to hold calls to Eva's room until after the service.

At a few minutes before three, Eva and I left the room. We were waiting in the lobby when the Cookes arrived.

'You and the children go on ahead,' she said to Sy, 'I want to ride alone.'

'Let her do what she wants,' Sy said to Carla, not acknowledging Eva. He wore a black cowboy hat.

'Now!' she said, sharply, holding back her tears. 'Go on. I have to go back to the room. I left my veil.'

The family followed her to the elevator cage.

'I should be crying and moaning and blubbering, I suppose,' she said, her eyes now filling once more with tears. 'But I'm all cried out. I just want it over with.'

She got into the elevator cage, giving us no chance to respond. It began to rise, leaving us below.

'Oh, I don't know,' Eva said, her hands clutching the cage as it rose. 'One minute I'm fine, steady and then it comes over me. She's ridden like that since she was a girl. We used to swim in the ditch and dive off the horses.'

Soon we were in a procession on our way out of town, up to the mesa on the west, opposite the college. Eva rode in a limousine behind the hearse. Then came Father Howard in his car and the Cookes and me in the gold van.

Eva seemed prepared now to take the day's events as if she moved along in a cloud or on a conveyer, confronting the coffin, the green awning and carpet, the preacher, the words spoken before the cold earth beside the grave, to accept it all, as each would appear before her.

At one point a white truck fell in line. Father Howard motioned for it to pass, but the driver stayed behind the Cooke van and turned on the headlights. When the procession arrived at the cemetery, the hearse went to the grave. The man driving the truck was Price Jones, the laundryman.

He remained behind in the parking lot while the Cooke family went first to May DuVal's marker next to Kate's grave. The place was without trees. Stark, barren except for the gravestones, the split-rail fence. The earth in front of May's marker had sucked back level with the ground. The rain had washed the sharp white rocks clean, and scattered tufts of brown grass and clots of wild flowers had been killed by the freeze. The topsoil was thin, and a gouge, a covered hole took years to vanish completely. Even after four years, the scars left by the shovels and pick-axes showed on the chunks of white limestone rock, fresh-looking scars, new, as if recently made. All that protected, all that covered Kate's aunt May was gravel, rock and sand — no peat or black dirt, no blanket of rotting leaves. Soon that would be true for Kate.

Ben left Kate's grave and approached the laundryman.

'Who do you think did it to her?' Price Jones asked.

'It was an accident,' said Ben. 'She was thrown by Aikin's horse, the roan.'

'The paper said she was a relative of Carla's. I didn't know that. Why didn't you say something when you were in the laundry the other day with that flyer?'

'You were busy,' said Ben. 'I was in a hurry.'

'I didn't look at it until yesterday. I knew her. We had beers a few times. Kate DuVal. She didn't drink beer. She liked tequila. Sunrises. That's what she drank.' He paused. 'I liked her. I liked her a lot, in fact. Is that her mother?'

'Yes. That's Eva.'

'I don't suppose she's up for company. I mean, I'd like to tell her how sorry I am. Kate was popular. She must have gone out with a lot of guys. I had to break it off with her.'

'If you want, I'll tell her a friend of Katie's is here.'

'I'd appreciate it, man. I just want to tell her I'm sorry. I mean, I feel bad, you know. She was nice, Kate was. I mean, I really liked her. I didn't hurt her, Ben.'

'I know you didn't.'

'It's a shock. I don't know what to do.'

'Let me ask Eva.'

'I can't settle down,' said Price. 'Ever since I heard, I haven't stopped shaking. It's like I've got the DT's or something. I mean maybe I was the last guy who was with her. Maybe I said something. Maybe I should have stayed with her longer. I don't know, man. She was putting the pressure on me. She wanted more than I

could give. It's just, it's just, I don't know, man, I'm
sorry.'

Eva waited by the hearse until it was time to follow the
men carrying the black coffin. They rested it on three
wide straps so it could be lowered into the grave. Then
the bearers stood away, by the backhoe.

Price Jones, at Ben's signal, approached Eva. She
looked up at him. She did not lift her veil as he joined
her under the awning on the green carpet and stood
next to her looking at Kate's coffin.

'So you're one of them?' she asked him, speaking
quietly now, but not looking at him. 'One of her men.'

'Yes, Ma'am,' he said. 'I believe I saw her last.'

'Damn you!' Eva's voice was sharp. Price Jones stepped
back. Her eyes flashed behind her veil. 'I will never
forget what you did to her, what all of you did to her,'
Eva said. 'Never, never, never.'

I made a move to grab Eva, but Sy took my arm. It
was all over. It had happened in a flash and left us all
stunned. Suddenly, Eva was quiet, amazed, I think, by
her rage.

'Leave her be,' Sy said. 'It's her right.'

Price Jones stepped away from her and he kept away
from the rest of the family now, but he stayed on for the
service of this nineteen-year-old girl — Kate DuVal,
daughter of Eva, cousin to Carla, student of Ben, and
Sy's protege on the guitar — this promising young girl,
as Father Howard intoned as he read the service, who
was cut down by accident.

'O Lord, may she dwell in Your house forever and rest
there in eternal peace: we beg of You, O Lord, to have
mercy upon this young woman's poor immortal soul
and to take her into the safety and goodness of Your
love.'

Father Howard was almost singing his lament for
her. He looked into the sky now; stretched his arms

toward the tall white tower of clouds above the mountains; told the six mourners and the three workmen and the pallbearers from the mortuary how Kate's loss was like the ten o'clock sun gone black, how it was like a river suddenly empty, like the young tree ripped of its unripe fruit, the set bud torn.

Then a rose was tossed by each of us. The coffin was lowered into the grave. And Eva asked me to take her back to the hotel.

'I couldn't bear one more word from that half-assed preacher,' she said.

As we walked toward the parking lot we heard the hollow sound of the rocks and gravel striking her daughter's coffin.

The frost line was almost a foot at the cemetery; below that the ground was soft and mostly gravel. The backhoe had brought out large chunks of frozen earth as large as pieces of heaved road. Those would go in last and stick out of the grave like dark half-buried blocks of asphalt, crumbling only when the ground thawed.

I helped Eva into the back seat of the limousine. Before we left, she asked me for a cigarette. She lifted her veil then and placed the cigarette between her lips, looking at me unwaveringly in the eyes while I held a light to the tip, and she almost smiled when she exhaled, diverting the smoke from my face. My hands were shaking.

'You loved her, Graden, didn't you?'

I nodded, my eyes filmed with tears.

'Eva,' I said, 'She. . . .' But I couldn't tell her. 'Eva, she . . . she was . . . looking for me.'

'I know,' Eva said. 'Yes, I know what she was.'

Then Eva moved slightly closer to me and when I reached out to touch her cheek, she kissed my palm. She was looking at me when a wave of pain went through her and her face turned cruel with grief.

As we drove away, the driver said something calming

which made us both turn for a last look up the hill. I did not look away from Kate's grave until it was out of sight.

After the first snow storm of winter, I moved here into Kate's trailer and began looking after Flame. It snowed again, a light fluffy powder which accumulated like goose down on the pine boughs and on the roof of the trailer and the barn. It bunched like froth on the frozen pasture and rose like sea foam in front of my boots. It snowed off and on for two weeks.

The world was quiet then, except for an occasional muffled car's exhaust and the sharp wind in the pines up by Joe Aikin's house and the squeal of snow under my boots on the shoveled path to Flame's barn and the rasping now and then of chains in the fender wells of passing trucks.

At the trailer this winter almost eight feet has accumulated, more has fallen than anyone living can remember. In the mountains fifteen feet of it is covering the lake, making this past winter the darkest and most severe in current memory and for many the longest and most silent.